The City
in
Crimson
Cloak

The City
in
Crimson
Cloak

by Asli Erdogan
Translated by Amy Spangler

Soft Skull Press • Brooklyn NY • 2007

The City in Crimson Cloak
Originally published in the Turkish language as *Kırmızı Pelerinli Kent*
© 1998 by Asli Erdogan

translation © 2007 by Amy Spangler

IBSN: 1-933368-74-8
ISBN 13: 978-1-933368-74-0

Book Design by Luke Gerwe

Published by Soft Skull Press
55 Washington St, Suite 804
Brooklyn NY 11201
www.softskull.com

Printed in the USA

Library of Congress-in-Publication Data available from the Library of Congress.

For Eduardo, who was killed by a stray bullet in Santa Teresa...

YOU were my death
You I could hold
When all fell away from me.
—Paul Celan

A TRAVELER
IN
THE STREETS OF RIO I

The people of Rio call their city, "the most beautiful place in the world." A choir reciting in unison: "The most beautiful place in the world..." This sentiment has been expressed in a variety of tongues in various forms, from tourist handbooks to exotically spiced films, from the conquistadores of the past to the carnival tourists of today who come to visit in package tours. And I agree – although I don't really know how they conceive of this thing called "the world," I do believe I've seen enough of it.

Here's a familiar, ordinary, breathtaking photograph of Rio for you: shadowless beaches of sparkling silver, stretching out into infinity, the labyrinthine shores of the Guanabara Gulf extending into the heart of the city... Mountains, like daggers thrust into the earth, rip the horizon to shreds; staggering abysses; magnificent, murderous, raging mad rock cliffs... Pao de Açucar (Sugar Loaf) Mountain sculpted out of a single piece of granite—on some days I liken it to a thumb, on others to a gravestone. Having preserved its mysteries for thousands of years the jungle, despite the many ravages it has endured, still a virgin bubbling with the fervency of adolescence... Beneath that piercing light of the tropics and reddish mist embracing the slopes, a city transformed into a land of fairytales...

I won't compose yet more odes in praise of Rio's exalted beauty, which has been described in significant detail. And in any case, I haven't had anything to do with Rio for a long time now. Suffice to say that the oldest image of the city in my memory is precisely that of this photograph, and that I saw it for the first time on a poorly printed, three cent postcard. In a word, I was enchanted. It was the rocks that impressed me most; contemporaries of the earth itself, ash gray, bronze, copper, violet, brick colored rocks standing there like sculptures of a lethal motion... Had I been of a more sentimental cast, I would have burnt the postcard in the flame of a candle and cast the ashes into the valley of Santa Teresa, from whence the gunshots rang out. But I, I just lost it.

The only thing I can do now is to wish those destined for the most beautiful city in the world a journey sans mishap or misfortune. I remind them that all adventures in Brazil have a bloody ending, that since the 16th century these savage lands have gotten the better of every voyager, harum scarum, gold hunter, and daringly mad-hearted soul to set foot upon them. I advise them not to forget for a single moment Rio's record highs in AIDS and crime statistics, under no circumstances to wander about by themselves, not to wear a watch, gold, or any jewelry that resembles gold, and to take every kind of rational precaution to keep the blood of the city from splattering upon them. And also to watch the sun set —an impressive but short-lived spectacle in the tropics— from Corcovado (that hill with the famous, gigantic statue of Jesus), and most definitely to try the fresh papaya juice...

And then there is the Rio of journalists, international aid organizations, human rights advocates, organizations "without borders." This is a city a third of whose population lives on the verge of starvation, a city up to its ears in crime, a city which grows fat from its trade in cheap mulatto flesh, cocaine, and arms. All six hundred of its hills have been appropriated by the favelas, and hundreds of thousands of homeless people are scattered upon its streets like so many rusty nails. A place of wholesale murder; reckless executions and meningitis and AIDS epidemics; Candelária Cathedral, with its garden where street children face the firing squad; gangs of Uzi-armed robbers raiding the beaches; "justiceiros" (purveyors of justice!) who don't know enough arithmetic to even keep a tally of the people they have killed... Well-intentioned, munificent, and credulous organizations trying to protect (from whom?) a people overworked, underfed, exploited to the very marrow of their bones... With a devilish wink Rio laughs them all off. She knows that they will be quick to give in, that once their consciences have chalked up a point or two, they will return to the infinitely boring First World, which, working with the efficiency of a wound-up clock, is as consistent in rationing out pain as it is in doling out pleasure. Packed full of mosquito bites, intestinal parasites, and memories of quick fixes, high convenience, hygienic adventures... As for those not yet satiated, she watches with great amusement as they, worn to a frazzle, escape to Nicaragua or to the Zapatista legions. That elusive, frivolous, flirtatious trickster, Rio!

The magnificent Rio photograph and its negative are a pair of masks, nothing more; only two of the many and varied costumes that the city, home of the carnival tradition for hundreds of years, has bedecked itself in. The Rio that I am going to tell you about, however, is a labyrinth established on more than two dimensions, or, to be more exact, a series of labyrinths interconnecting on the planes of time and space. Full of dead ends, blind spots, hidden rooms, frightening echoes, convulsive writhing, vague predictions...

In a little bit you will walk out onto the streets of Rio. This will be a journey within arrow range of a creature that makes its monstrosity felt at each and every moment; the stench of death's breath constantly in your face; eyes laden with darkness; perversity always just a step behind... As if you are leaning over a well and suddenly realize that the creature is stalking you... You will encounter the human body as an illicit gift intended to ingratiate, set upon the miserable throne of desire's realm. The idiocy, incomparable beauty, and inextinguishable fire of flesh; a light, volatile, fickle life, and a death at every corner...

It was two years ago. At a holiday celebration in the ghettos I saw a woman, wrapped in rags, her legs and backside completely exposed. (It took me several minutes to figure out which sex she was). She looked like someone who had been rescued too late from a concentration camp and was destined to perish within a matter of days. She could have been in her twenties, or just as well in her seventies. She was missing most of her teeth, and her elbows jutted out through her skin. She was doing the samba. Ecstatic with pleasure, roaring with laughter... Her face alight with that innocent, pure joy seen only on the faces of children... And so it is then, when you look into the hazy, foggy, bottomless eyes of a woman on the verge of death and you confront happiness, true happiness, that you will have plunged into the labyrinths of Rio. Henceforth, in return for what you see, you will pay in kind with your life. Just as I did.

And now what you—and I—need is a bit of courage. As much, perhaps, as you need before plunging into dark waters, or laying down your cards in a game of poker. Don't forget! It is Rio de Janeiro that you are up against. (Did you know that its name means "January River"?) A city grown so adept at the game of endless coincidences, even the devil is considered a mere amateur in comparison. The moment she makes you believe that she is bluffing, she whips out the ace of diamonds.

Now close your eyes. I'm going to silently count to ten. When I say ten, you will be in Rio. 'Tis a pity that I will not be telling you when you should open your eyes.

FIREWORKS DAY

Traveler, who are you?
What is it that you seek down there?
—Thus Spoke Zarathustra

She had finally succeeded in becoming a real vagabond, having upped and disappeared into this South American city famous for its murders of street children, and its carnival. Indeed, she had turned out to be one of the millions of cast-about drifters on this planet, one of the lost souls left to the mercy of iron-fisted fate. An adventure-loving gal from a good family, the once small, delicate, frightened young girl has now become a consummate rogue. She no longer falls for fairytales, she can walk the streets alone at night, and she doesn't brag about the beatings she takes. Here in this vicious city, sprawled upon the ground as if her intestines have been ripped to pieces, not even in the thought of death does she find solace.

She had crossed oceans, traversed the equator, and set foot upon a piece of land about which she knew absolutely nothing. Everything she left behind, she had fed to the flames. And what confronted her upon her arrival was a universe defiled and debased to the core. The old ways of the Old World no longer applied. Value judgments were now like the heavy, useless piece of luggage she had carried over from Turkey. Its bottom worn and scruffy, its handle about to come off, it's been left to rot away in the dampness of the tropics. Abandoned until that continuously deferred return.

When the life-defying girl chose "the world's most danger-ous" city, her sole intention had been to glance into the depths of humankind. To look from a safe distance... Instead, her hair went up in flames in this hell that she faced of her own volition. Rio de Janeiro sicced its stupefying anarchy upon her, its days of white heat,

its nights full of promises, threats, caresses, its murders... Its will now
bereft of its muscle power, its individuality hanging off of it in tatters.
An army that has been routed and left its wounded behind...

The sound of gunfire started up again all at once; a startled Özgür
jumped, and the glass in her left hand fell to the floor. Her entire body tensed and began shaking, as if she had been given an
electrical shock. Sweat was gushing from every pore of her body,
but at the same time she was freezing cold. Caustic tears welled
up in her eyes yet failed to flow. "Enough! Enough! I can't take it
anymore! My God, put an end to this torture, now! Can't you see
that I've no strength left?"

Her nervous attack lasted only two or three minutes before
she gathered herself together again. With the attentiveness of an
expert, she listened to the monologue of the semi-automatic. As
soon as she understood that the gunfire was coming not from the
favelas—as ghettos are called in Brazil—but from the valley right
next to her, she decided to go inside. It relieved her to see that
not one glass was cracked, and that not a single drop of tea had
spilled onto her notebooks. When she realized, what's more, that
the sweaty fingers of her right hand had tightly clung to her pen
throughout the duration of the attack, she smiled.

The two huge *favelas* located on Santa Teresa Hill, on the slope
leading down to the jungle, had been at war for eight days. Since
the junta period, around six hundred of the *favelas*, which had
turned Rio's extraordinarily beautiful face into a massive pock-
mark, had been under the control of Commando Verelho, one of
Latin America's most powerful criminal organizations. Every day
was riddled with conflict; competing gangs would rip into one
another over the division of cocaine shares, or the police, dissat-
isfied with their own kickbacks, would carry out raids in units of
fifty, armed to the teeth.

Who would've guessed that the worst war that Özgür was to see during her two years in Rio would break out in Santa Teresa. Since last Saturday, the sound of infantry guns, Uzis, and hand grenades had ushered in the day and continued throughout. Two nights ago, she was in Santa Teresa, famous for its bars, and as she wandered its deadly silent streets lined with defunct lamp lights, Özgür saw half a dozen buses—their headlights dimmed, crammed full of soldiers, long barrels hanging out of their windows—silently climb up the hill. But rather than put an end to the conflict, the army's intervention had sent it spinning out of control.

Until just the day before, she had always considered the sound of the gunshots to be just another noise amongst many in the non-stop commotion of Rio, just another blemish that kept her from concentrating on her novel, or so that's how she thought she considered it. Until the nervous attacks began...

She was trying to determine exactly how this period of no return had begun. If she could only draw the borders and lay out its touchstones, then at least perhaps she could bring it under the control of her mind. If she had to choose a point zero, she would choose the day that she encountered the mulatto woman in Copacabana. The final day of Easter, when all the clocks in Rio stopped, when the heat suddenly shot up to over forty degrees, when the city began to shake as if gripped by jungle fever...

It was Sunday. Just an ordinary Sunday... another day exactly like the ones preceding it, days swiftly passing, devoid of hope, expectation, or meaning, full of nothing but an insipid emptiness... Fireworks Day...

Although it was the first week of December, the horrid heat of Rio de Janeiro had swept over the city wave after wave like a rising ocean tide. And so it was to be for weeks, months, the temperature never dropping below forty Celsius, as if the street thermometers scattered all over the city were being held in the armpit of a yellow fever patient: 42, 41.5, 43, 43.6, 42.4... In Rio, shut off from the ocean winds by jagged coves and precipitous mountains, not a leaf budges during the months of the so-called "dry season," nor is its radiant, indigo blue sky stained by a single cloud. Heat descends upon you like madness, wraps itself around your throat, chokes you. The city becomes a huge furnace slowly roasting human bodies alive. The sun removes the benevolent queen mask that it had worn all year and behaves like a dictator consumed by the desire to kill. The air absorbs all the humidity it can and thickens to the consistency of water. That famous humidity of the tropics...

Now instead of a *salgadinho*—a small bread-like pastry—the street kids beg for a cola. And so henceforth will they die of dysentery, cholera, or downright dehydration. All of the city's fountains dry up, and the bodies of the homeless emit an even ranker stench, and because the open-air toilets on the sidewalks where they dwell cease to be cleaned by the rains, the smell of feces, urine, and rot pervades the streets. Vendors pack up the sweets called *bombons*, their chocolate-covered cashews, their banana fruit rolls, and replace them with cold beverages and fresh coconut juice. "*Gelada, gelada...*" ("Ice-cold, Ice-cold...") The people of the city are drained of their strength; paces, conversations, even breathing, slow down as life struggles to take its course, lurching along like a river that's beginning to dry up. Conversations in passing, on elevators, in waiting rooms, on buses, all begin with the same sentence: *Que calor!* (What heat!) From the colorful advertising posters plastered all over Rio, Scandinavian-looking girls in knee-high snow scatter twinkling, blonde, infantile smiles. Just as the Bedouins have a passion for green, in the hearts of the people of Rio lies a passion for snow.

By the first Sunday of December, the people of the city had already either scrambled to the beaches or escaped to the mountain villages. Time had nearly come to a standstill. The hours slowly lost their grip, drip-dropping away like beads of sweat. In the Santa Teresa valley, which had otherwise withdrawn into a deep siesta, gangs savagely exchanged shots.

Özgür's home consisted of a long and narrow trough-like living room, a kitchen that she had named "the coffin cell," and a bathroom full of leeches that she just couldn't bring herself to kill because it made her so nauseous. It was one of six studio apartments in the grandiloquently named "White Villa," pretentious columns and all. The slope looking onto the Santa Teresa valley was so steep that while the balcony in front was at least three meters above the ground, the windows in back were at ground level and opened onto a jungle full of weeds and thorny bushes. Carnivorous ants, lizards, grasshoppers, winged cockroaches the size of a hand, and sometimes even ravenous wild cats would suddenly barge in through the windows, which she had to keep open day and night because of the heat. Once she herself jumped out the window and tried to make her way through the jungle, but her hands and face were covered in cuts and scratches before she even made it two steps. Although she knew that no animal larger than a cat could possibly make it over those bushes, the nocturnal noises coming from the garden scared her senseless. She didn't have the money to purchase a fan. Though revoltingly rich, her miserly swindler of a landlord, Professor Botelho, had deprived his renters of air-conditioning, which was as vital here as central heating is in Stockholm. He was the right-wing mayor's chief advisor; he lorded his highbrow education and unadulterated European roots over others, and would go to great lengths to assume a noble air and the elite mannerisms befitting the dignity of his forefathers. Moreover, he was a neat freak; he worshipped rules, order, design. He had adorned the side of the building looking onto the garden with Greek gods of smooth marble, lamps reeking of Paris, and an elegant staircase that glided down through the banana and mango trees. The apartment furnishings were yet another concrete expression of his gilded personality. Into Özgür's living room were piled a huge ugly bed hard as concrete, aluminum bookshelves, a fake leather chair-couch mongrel that looked like it had been pilfered from city hall, and in the middle of all this rubbish had been placed a heavy, elaborately decorated mahogany table together with eight chairs that occupied an excessive amount of space. And then there was the hammock, the sine qua non of Rio houses, which had been strung across the balcony; strings of shells hanging from the door tintinnabulated at the hint of the slightest breeze. (According to a Brazilian belief of African origin, sea shells bring good luck.) On the gray walls, reminiscent of hospital or courthouse corridors, hung a black and white poster that Prof. Botelho had bought from the New York Metropolitan and had so very meticulously framed. A close-up photo of the slightly oily-looking parted lips of a kissing couple... Once upon a time she had found the dull, hazy, virtually official eroticism of it titillating. Especially on those nights when, in the high-pressure, suffocating atmosphere of the house, she perceived her loneliness to be a being outside of herself, a being heavy like mercury, growing like suds, bubble by bubble, spinning out of control, approaching the point of explosion... On those nights, she wanted to press her lips against those of the tie-bedecked man in the photograph. Not to kiss though, no, more like a hungry chick reaching out to its mother's beak.

Here I am in this semi-savage land, all alone, an unfamiliar feeling of being both free and besieged brewing within me. (Lonely, alone, derelict, vagrant, orphaned... I can list any number of adjectives, but I cannot build a bridge between words and reality.) The absolute, impeccable, infernal freedom of having not a single person who needs me, or anyone looking after me... I can brandish the lies of my choice, fabricate the past that I long for, pursue the most sinful of fantasies. Once I've ensured a slick getaway out the back door, I'm capable of committing the most abominable of crimes. I read in a book once that if you open the door of a canary's cage, the canary instantly makes a dash for the window. Yet when the window, too, is opened, the canary makes what is—according to the author—the wisest choice by return-ing to its cage, and thus escaping certain death.

Sometimes I pursue a fractured memory to the other side of the Atlantic. The contours of the past fade away and disappear in the raw light of the tropics. The ocean, that petulant, stormy, immortal ocean has vanquished all of my seas. The screams of parrots now offer more evocations than the sound of seagulls.

Giving up steeped tea for filtered coffee, wrestling with the waves of the Atlantic rather than striking out upon the waters of a calm, humble inland sea, dreaming in a Latin language... These are changes that I could overcome, but there were also losses that could never be replaced. I'm not referring to whims such as white cheese, sage tea, or the Bosphorus. My longings are much simpler than that. For ex-ample, cherries... Sometimes I lie in bed and imagine a bowl of dark red cherries covered in a thin layer of ice. An erotic fantasy of sorts. So plain, uncomplicated, raw. I miss the changing of the seasons. How the leaves adorn themselves first with streaks of red and then burst into flame before slowly roasting in the heat of an internal fire... How one morning they suddenly fall feeble and float to the ground... Walking without a thought as to my destination, with purple lips and the northeast wind whipping at my face... That incomparable first, bitter sip of tea when the cold becomes unbearable. In the heat of this infernal February, I even miss the snow, which I have always despised. The snowy beech forests, tundra, steppes that I have never seen... The thermometer hasn't dipped below forty in six weeks and the air reeks of leather jackets. And then... I miss walking as I please, without hiding my watch in my bag, without clinging to my purse and constantly watching my back, without fearing a handgun that could be pressed to my forehead at any moment... Sleep eviscerated by the sound of gunshots... My eyes are always wide open, I'm always alert, I smoke one cigarette after the other, but no matter what I do, I cannot stop the constant trembling of my lips.

But for all of this, I have made some gains, too. I do not, for example, have to carry an ID, the bars that I go to are open until morning, nobody notices that I don't wear a bra; in fact, I don't wear any underwear on days when it's over forty degrees. I have pleated skirts that ride my ass, tight shorts, and thongs, and I like to watch my body in its belatedly acquired femininity. I revel in the feel of my hair, which hasn't been touched by scissors in a year, scampering along my back like wild colts. (If this city weren't so windless, if I could have shaken off, for just one moment, my anxiety at the prospect of being dishonest, then I would have written of how much I enjoyed the feeling of my hair "being tousled by the wind." But Rio is windless... It doesn't breathe, that is, it lacks a spirit.) I can dance in restaurants, bars, on sidewalks, smoke on buses, and sleep with any man I want. Here I am allowed to indulge in the most vulgar of my desires to my heart's content. I could even hire an assassin, if I could come up with four hundred bucks. Or could it be that I miss those millstones of the Old World, millstones which are part and parcel, perhaps the very buttress, of my self?

Fly back to your cage, little canary, fly back to your cage! While you still have time... For that open window is your abyss!

She found this text while flipping through some old notebooks, tucked between her topology notes and Portuguese verb conjugations. She must have written that passage during her first dry season in the tropics. She was fond of that innocence of sorts, which she had by now long ago lost, that childish naïveté concealed beneath her whimpering. "I never have been able to overcome my loneliness," she thought. "But it seems like I have grown outwards from it—grown enough that I can wrap myself around it. It is like a fetus within me now, like a medal I wear upon my chest."

She was sitting at the table before her notebook, in front of her a beer glass full of Brazilian tea that, no matter how long it was left to brew, never grew darker than the color of straw; lost in thought, she was chewing on the pen that had become an extension of her very body, a third, prosthetic hand. She felt the room's airless heat work slowly into her body, unraveling and diffusing. Her breathing became erratic, her thoughts chaotic, like blind bats. A new wave of sweat covered her body with each sip she took. She could detect the acrid smell of her underarms, the annoying straps of the house dress clinging to her body, the taste of cheap tobacco in her mouth... "Point Zero" definitely had to be written before the day was through.

Just then she noticed that the gunfire in the valley had ceased and been replaced by the *favelas'* favorite rap song blasting out of a boom box. *"Ele era um bandito mas era um bom rapaz..."* ("He was a bandit, but he was a good guy...") She was amazed to find that the song, a wonder of shallowness, penetrated her heart, and that its past tense in particular caused her great pain. She grieved the death of this bandit whom she did not know. The voice of the negro singing the song was deep and sorrowful, and it smelled of gunpowder... It arose from the land of semi-automatics where deaths are a dime a dozen, and Özgür knew well and good that the singer, like her own friend, was one of the good guys, the bandits, who didn't have long to live. A memory from memory's many sarcophagi... Another song... Another heart-rending song... She began turning the pages of *The City in Crimson Cloak*.

FIRST DAY IN RIO

Rio had welcomed her with foggy weather and a lead gray sky, which immediately threw her for a loop, for she had struck out on her journey full of tropical dreams. She'd plopped herself into a taxi, teetering on the edge, exhausted after eighteen sleepless hours of flight, and listened disinterestedly to the driver. Like a parrot the man repeated over and over in dreadful English, "Rio is the most beautiful place, the most beautiful place." She had just lit a cigarette when they hit the favelas. Thousands, no, tens of thousands of decrepit houses piled on top of one another, extending for miles, all the way to downtown Rio. Roofless cabins, shanties of brick, cardboard, tin, labyrinths sunk knee-deep in a sea of mud...

It didn't take long for Rio to teach her its first lesson; no longer than it took her to smoke her first cigarette. The land upon which she had been born and raised had protected her from falling off one of life's cliffs, into the ghastly depths of squalor into which humankind sometimes descends. It was beyond anything she could have imagined. A powerful sense of foreboding whispered that she was on a train that had run off its track and was hurtling forward at full speed, that this city which fed on human suffering would be the end of her. However, they quickly reached downtown, followed by "the most beautiful place in the world," Copacabana, and it was then that Rio de Janeiro took her captive, with its coves of stunning beauty, its savage cliffs, its tropical revelry. She forgot all about the favelas. In a snap, just like that—and just like the middle class citizens of Rio did, too.

She had gone to the only address she knew in Brazil, to her professor's apartment. They had let her know right away that she wasn't wanted; they didn't even give her a room. Hours later, they took pity on the pale-faced foreigner who'd fallen asleep in a chair and told her that for the time being she could sleep in the somber servant's room opening onto the courtyard.

It was dark out when the sound of drums awoke her. She couldn't figure out where she was. Was she in Istanbul, or on the plane? The sound of a dozen drums playing out a rhythm so jubilant, so peerless, so extraordinary that it brought tears to one's eyes... A penetrating, melancholy male voice broke out in song. The voice had to belong to a negro, and it must have been coming from the fringes of the city. It seemed to be familiar with all of the gutters, the quagmires, the snaps of the whip that life serves up. And that's when it hit her—they were in the tropics. She was standing on the edge of an ocean, on the threshold to a completely different life. She was in Rio de Janeiro. She immediately wanted to take the first plane back home. But that voice! She felt a strong desire to run barefoot into the future; an urge to draw her sword and run her horse at full gallop, straight into the formidable front battle line of life... This, she thought, was probably what they meant by "joie de vivre."

She downed the last dregs of her tea like a true Bavarian. Her thirst hadn't subsided at all. On days when the temperature rose above thirty-seven, it didn't matter how much fluid she drank, her tongue remained like sandpaper. It was as if everything she drank went straight to her stomach, without even so much as scraping her palate. She had never before experienced such thirst, a thirst that was unique to the tropics. "This tea just isn't doing the trick," she grumbled. "I need something cold; watermelon, or a *guaraná* soda."

She knew perfectly well that warm tea was better relief in this heat than a cold soda. She had learned the hard way just which rules one must follow to make it through the dry season in one piece, like drinking a half pint of water every half hour. Delicate and capricious, her mis-created body did not befit her intrepid soul. Her Caucasian blood, with a drop or two of Mediterranean water mixed in, had given her a ghostly white skin that moaned bitterly beneath Rio's cruel sun, a nearly translucent skin of the type that the negroes called "newspaper colored." Asthma attacked her constantly on the dust-bathed streets, and because of allergies caused by vermin, she itched all over day and night, as if thousands of ants were storming up and down her body. Her stomach couldn't handle the acidic tropical fruits, or the oily Brazilian food. And what's worse, she'd really given herself free rein, turning a deaf ear to all warnings, eating and drinking at food stands that smelled of urine in neighborhoods where all kinds of epidemics, from meningitis to AIDS, ran rampant, and so she had been infected by amoebas and invaded by intestinal parasites time and time again.

Her kitchen had been under the occupation of fruit flies and ants for some time; cans of corn with a nasty liquid oozing out of them were strewn right and left. She opened the refrigerator, more to cool off than to look and see what was inside. There was nothing but coffee, a piece of Minas cheese—a distant South American relative of Turkish white cheese—that was starting to turn yellow, and two lemons that were starting to spoil. She hadn't been shopping for probably ten days at least. She turned on the mud clogged filter that had been left behind by the previous renter, awkwardly wielded a hammer, and began to break off pieces of ice from the freezer. As she struck at the ice, all of a sweat, she grew angry with herself once again for not having bought an ice tray or a filter in all the months she'd been there, cursing her incorrigible "couldn't care less" attitude. She placed lots of ice and some sweetener in a glass of lemonade; she turned to go to the living room with her drink, which was in no way sufficient reward for her efforts. She was covered in sweat and had already lost more liquid in acquiring her drink than the drink itself contained. She lit a cigarette and deposited herself upon the fake leather couch.

The salvo of automatic guns had ceased, and the syncopated rhythm of an indolent pistol took its place. Three or four shots, silence, three or four more... Shots of a weary gunman with no intention of killing, just unable to endure the silence. The conflicts in Rio were nothing like those that she had seen in the movies. Banditos did not lavishly rain down bullets like the ruthless, bold, superhuman Hollywood gangsters; they were frugal, they took their time. One day, during her second month in Rio, she was sitting in front of a theater pretending to listen to the street actors' conversation when she suddenly found herself caught in the crossfire, wedged between some madly dashing car thieves and the police in hot pursuit. Experienced *Cariocas*, as the people of Rio called themselves, immediately threw themselves to the ground; Özgür meanwhile leapt to her feet, cigarette in one hand and *guaraná* soda in the other, and with the curiosity of a child getting her first glimpse at a piranha, stared after the car robber, who was hanging out the front window from his waist, firing nonstop. She expected his eyes to be huge, covering nearly all of his face and full of dread like those of a game animal. But his face expressed not even a hint of fear. In fact, his face expressed nothing. Like an arrow unleashed from the bow, the man concentrated intently upon one thing: Hitting the bull's eye. The only things he had with which to stop the car of death trailing after him were a gun and steady fingers. And maybe the amulet he never failed to take to work with him in the mornings... The more intense it became, the more his fear of death must have been fading away; much like unhappiness does. Roberto grabbed Özgür by the waist, yanking her to the ground and saving her life.

She picked up a copy of *O Globo*, which, including the Sunday inserts, weighed in at over one hundred pages, hoping to find something that she had not yet read. Column after column of celebrity news; love and romance, gossip, soccer, dispassionate articles on politics, hackneyed, frivolous op-eds, astrology, personality tests... prostitution ads... mulatto panthers, blonde, blue-eyed "European types," whip-bearing Amazons... An engraving of Rio in loud colors and distorted perspective, wreaking utter chaos... The city would usually request a third page since the twenty murders that—according to government statistics—occurred each day did not fit on the two pages already devoted to "Violence." Özgür would scour those news items, taking down notes with a statistician's meticulous passion for bare facts. Journalists who'd had their tongues cut out and their ears cut off, housewives who'd been riddled with bullets because they dared to hold onto their purses, street children castrated and then murdered by the police... The chilling stories, packed into only three or four sentences, moved her profoundly. She identified both with the murder victims as well as with the gangsters who were captured by the police. And she also sensed that, deep inside, she derived a kind of perverted, highly criminal pleasure from it all. In Rio she had tasted the erotic in human blood. What's more, there was some kind of relief in knowing the dreadful dimensions of the pit of quicksand into which she sank. Death, when reduced to numbers, ceased to be personal tragedy.

Maria de Penha (41): Caught in the midst of an armed conflict on the bus; while the rest of the passengers threw themselves to the floor, she was squished to death in the turnstile.

Another Maria (13): She skipped school and went to the beach, where she was shot in the head by a stray bullet; the autopsy revealed that the girl was pregnant. Both her killer and the father of her baby remain unknown.

An interview with street kid Joao (9):

— Your favorite book?

— *My first grade reading book. I've never read any other books.*

— *People you admire?*

— *Pele, Romario, Ayrton Senna.*

— *Your best feature?*

— *I protect girls living on the streets. I don't beat them.*

— *Your worst feature?*

— *... (Pauses)... I guess... robbery.*

— *Who do you want to be like?*

— *I've never known anybody... good enough to look up to.*

The weather report said that it would be thirty-seven degrees, sunny with clear skies in Rio. In Istanbul meanwhile it was to be two degrees with snowfall. "If I were over there, I'd be wanting some *salep*," thought Özgür. She'd just finished off her lemonade, but the rusty taste in her mouth remained.

Towards the end of November, the language school where she gave English lessons let out for summer vacation. This also put an end to the miniscule sense of order and duty that had given Özgür's days, which otherwise dangled in a void of nothingness, some semblance of structure, much like the bandages that hold a mummy together. And so now she almost never set foot outside her house unless absolutely necessary. She spent two days a week giving private lessons. From the break of dawn through to the middle of the night she chased after students who were constantly shirking class, canceling without letting her know ahead of time, and straight up vanishing; it was usually a struggle wheedling unpaid bills out of the debtors, and she had to resort to methods completely inconsistent with her personality, everything from threats to fawning and flattery. The following day she would wake up around noon, and then only with the greatest difficulty. After an uneasy sleep constantly interrupted by nightmares, slumber that was more like thrashing for her life in a bubbling swamp, she would find herself drenched in sweat and more exhausted than she had been when she first got into bed; her eyelids would be glued to her eyes, stubbornly refusing to open. She never remembered her dreams, but she knew that every night—*every* night—she wept quietly, sobbed silently. The tears she shed then were her truest, her most sincere. For several minutes she would be unable to tell where she was—in fact, *who* she was—and she would rub her eyes, dazzled by the piercing noontime sun, and try to return to reality. Or perhaps she wouldn't try, for in the end, a reality even more horrible than the most horrendous nightmare would cruelly seek her out. She would then recall with infallible certainty that she was in Rio de Janeiro, and sighing more deeply than usual, she would sit up before making her way to the kitchen, all the while spewing a litany of Turkish profanities, her mouth tasting like an ashtray. Once she'd placed the teapot on the stove, she'd walk back and like an empty potato sack collapse back down onto her wrinkled, smelly, damp sheets. First cigarette of the day... That first cigarette, filling her lungs with insidious, compassionate smoke, as she prepared to face another day determined to take another nick out of her soul...

A beer mug full of tea and two more cigarettes... Some more tea, some more cigarettes... Put on some fresh tea, open up another pack... Too lazy to empty out the two heaping full ashtrays from the previous night, she would slide over an empty can left over from the last night's dinner and lie down on the chaise-longue. Managing to think about absolutely positively nothing of any consequence whatsoever, avoiding any analysis or interpretation regarding her self, masterfully drawing a curtain over all of the decisions she had to make, she would stare at the wall, her eyes closed to the outside world. All of the hours belonged to her, but not to be used—to be spread out like a corpse in the eternal void that they contained. After several pots of tea and a pack of cigarettes, a cramp would enter her stomach and she would feel a pang much like that which accompanies the feeling of hunger, a feeling she could hardly recall anymore, and so she would eat a piece of Minas cheese with some of the flat bread they called "Arabian bread" in Brazil, just so she could continue smoking. She would spend an entire day in the chaise-longue, like a sentry who is under no circumstances to abandon his position, moving only to shift her weight just a bit when the pain in her tailbone became unbearable, with her glass and cigarettes always within arm's reach. If a person has strength to do nothing else; if she cannot even take her eyes off of a blind wall and reach out for a book; if she cannot turn to look at the banana trees or the wild jungle in the Santa Theresa valley; if she is in no condition to smile at her most innocent, cutest childhood memory or grow sentimental at sundown, then steeping tea and smoking cigarettes are vital activities. The lizard with which Özgür was sharing her house would stand motionless upon the "Kissing Lips" photograph all day long; as if lost in profound thought and with understanding eyes, it would take long lingering looks at Özgür, an enormous creature as silent and inanimate as itself. It was as if both of them had just collapsed at their final stop on this earth, sick and tired of the emptiness, of the banality of the world, hopeless and indifferent and utterly exhausted.

It was only at nightfall, when the neighbors' raucous television filled her cemetery with fake screams and laughter, that she managed to pull herself together. She ate a can of corn and plopped down in front of her novel. The night progressed; Adelino in apartment four cuddled his saxophone, the hopeless dream he'd been aspiring to for years; the dogs of Santa Theresa began to howl; the sounds of *pagoda*—a dance rhythm—and gunshots began to ring out from the *favelas*; the parrot of Joao in apartment six cussed and cursed in outrage at the cacophony. Finally, the sound of lovemaking coming from the floor right above her drowned out all the others. The laughter, moaning, and flailing of the women named Rosanna, Lucy, Katja, and Thais as they took their turns—the man was always the same, Marcello—enveloped her. Despite the exhibitions of these couples who, like all similar couples in Rio, are determined to prove to all mortal souls that sex is the most glorious pleasure to be had, LOVE had no place in her writings, did not even seep through in its most symbolic form. There was always DEATH on the white pieces of paper filled with scrawled letters, scribbling, arrows darting to the right and left. A death, constantly rearing its head, thrashing about in an effort to right itself, struggling with all of its might to rip through the web of blue ink above it... Amongst those circles and lines called the Latin alphabet it strove to come into being, to emerge from its flat, leveled, smoothed-over universe and seize another dimension.

"How to explain Rio de Janeiro?" she mumbled to herself. "Which Maria's story should I choose?" This city offered way too many spectacles, way too many contradictions, way too many tragedies. She was constantly running into freaks, torture wounds, corpses, and sex... The magnificent Ipanema beach lined with "the world's most expensive" apartments, and right behind it, the three hundred thousand person Rocinha, the world's largest *favela*, resembling the hunched back of a crippled person trying to right himself... Writing meant first and foremost putting things into order, and Rio, if it were to be defined in just one word, was CHAOS. Trying to capture it was like tracking an extremely cunning, predatory bird in a rainforest full of poisonous thorns, crocodiles, and anacondas. Which words—*whose* words?—could she use to describe hunger to a sophisticated, educated someone who had never experienced hunger, and who would be sinking down in a comfortable chair and doing the least risky occupation in the world—reading?

She thought of the foreigners tossed into tropical waters by the northern currents, caught in the net of Rio—a city which had devoured each and every prey that landed in its lap, easily grinding them to a pulp. European names inscribed in her memory, echoing all the sorrow of migration: Ronaldo, Mara, Lothar, Katja... They tended to their wounds in cool climates, unaware of the roles, large and small, that they had been given in Özgür's novel. Ronaldo, the playwright who marked each day that he had to spend in Rio off the calendar like a convict awaiting release... Because he was a devoted Buddhist and a true asexual, and because he never went to parties and he despised drinking, dancing, and noise, in theater circles he was considered to be stark raving mad. Before the first two months were even up he'd locked himself up in his empty room full of incense and sought therapy in the form of meditation. "Superficiality is in a state of epidemic all over the world, but in this city, it's a religion," he used to say. With nearly identical desperation Mara, too, had reached almost the same conclusion: "I've found superficiality everywhere I've set foot in the world, but here, it's become an art form." Mara was an anthropologist. She had spent five years traipsing around Central America, had fought in Nicaragua, and had lived with savage tribes in the jungle. Rio had managed to do in even this haughty, reserved academic, this harsh, steel-willed, no-holds-barred woman. After a love escapade that pushed her to the verge of suicide, she quit her study, entitled something like "Mulatto Ghetto Women in Brazil and Their Relationship with Their Own Bodies," halfway through and headed back to the dreary gray skies of her native London, now completely in doubt of her values. Poor Mara! She had been knocked out flat in a viciously real arena, much more real than that of any thesis or analysis or institution—the arena of the body. Another weathered Nicaraguan warrior named Lothar referred to his pre-Rio life as his "Age of Innocence." The licentiousness had swollen his ego to the verge of explosion. "This city sucks the willpower right out of ya!" he'd mumble mirthfully after each night of amour. The well-intentioned, small town beauty Katja became seriously depressed for the first time in her life after being seduced by a married man who then vanished into thin air. "Think only of yourself," she'd told Özgür, back when she was still quite innocent, quite the novice. "This city is lethal to foreign women. Learn to love yourself, because nobody else will." As a respite from their worthless loneliness, a feeling that could not possibly be shared, they'd embraced each other and taken refuge in the consolation of their mutual sympathies. (And this was a much more potent pain reliever than love, especially the only kind of love you could find in Rio, because it never wounded your pride.) They'd gone to great lengths to adapt to this congenial, capricious, indulgent city; they'd rushed to and fro, dashing from one concert, dance, political rally, *favela*, and most of all, promise of love, to the next. It was impossible to get your fill of consuming what in reality you did not need.

The telephone rang. Özgür flinched, like she did when the gunshots rang out, but she remained otherwise non-responsive. Her abstraction from the outside world had increased together with her loneliness; she had long ago quit running to answer every time that attention-hungry contraption squealed. What's more, thanks to Prof. Botelho's incomparable stinginess, she had to share a single line with five renters and all of their lovers, siblings, cousins, servants, etc. She looked at the constantly trembling receiver that croaked like a frog and was at least twenty years old, perhaps even one of the first models available in Brazil, and coolly calculated the possibilities. Her mother only called her on Sundays, fireworks day. What had started out as weekly phone calls two years ago had over time grown increasingly less frequent, and the teary-eyed conversations of longing had become caricatures of themselves. The caller also could have been any one of the countless men aged between fifteen and fifty who, having checked off all the names in their little black books on this dreariest of nights, had decided to try their luck with the cold semolina Turkish woman. She was so sick of calls to go out to dinner, to *domingueira*—Sunday dances—festas, bars, "*um chopinho*" ("one little beer"), or motels that she could almost puke. At the very worst it could be her landlord calling to "discuss the matter of her overdue rent," or Lizboa. She had met the latter, a happy-go-lucky lawyer from Copacabana, about a year and a half earlier when she still spoke only a smattering of Portuguese, when he dialed the wrong number. For some reason he'd become obsessed with Özgür. He'd call every Sunday and go on and on for at least an hour in monologues about his prudent success at work, his bedroom adventures, and his burgeoning young lovers, all the while emphasizing details such as how forty-nine people attended his birthday party, or how he had slept with five different women in the last three weeks, with all the philistinism of a nouveau riche. She knew the *Cariocas* well enough by then to know that he wasn't lying. She understood very well the loneliness of this veteran womanizer who was only able to open up to a woman whose face he had never seen; a loneliness concealed behind numbers, and which the owner tried to erase in crowds of idle onlookers and motel rooms rented out by the hour. Or maybe it was Eli... Could it really be Eli who was calling? No, impossible!

She made her decision at the last minute and, springing from the couch, grabbed the telephone just as apartment six's answering machine was about to pick up.

"*Quem está falando?*"

"Hello. I—want—to— talk—to—ÖZGÜR."

Her mother pronounced each word deliberately in heavily accented English, like an anchorwoman reading the news to the deaf and mute. Özgür felt a spark of true joy light up inside of her.

"Hi, mom."

"Hello, I want..."

"Mom, it's me! Don't you recognize my voice? Why haven't you called?"

She hadn't spoken Turkish in so long that her voice sounded odd to her now in her mother tongue. Like she was mumbling in her sleep. No matter how much her mother professed to the contrary, she was convinced that she had acquired a slight Brazilian accent, and that her diction was off as well.

"Is that you? Oh, good. That man, what's his name, Joa or something, he's always hanging up on me. I'm sorry I haven't been able to call for a while. I had to go down to our summer home; it got flooded. How are you?"

For several moments she was at a loss for words; finally, she let out an indifferent, "Same as always. And how are you? What are you up to?"

"I'm thinking of going to Moscow in January. Tours have gotten really cheap. I'm sorry, I can't talk too long. The phone bill last month cost me a good three million."

Özgür didn't respond. Her mother's words rained down upon her brain like transparent bullets. A steel hand had wrapped itself around her head and was yanking her forcefully to the ground. That familiar nausea...

"So what's up?" her mother continued, obviously struggling to find any questions to ask. "How are you feeling?"

"Awful. I'm not eating. I can't."

The truth is that she was hoping that her mother would be able to comprehend the vital difference between those last two sentences; she didn't.

"You've cut down on the smoking I hope."

"I don't keep track."

A prickly silence of porcupine proportions. The mother and daughter became aware of the Atlantic Ocean separating them. That they spoke without saying anything, so as not to say anything...

"What are you doing in that awful city anyway? Why haven't you come back yet? I mean, you're not even doing anything over there, just bumming around. You've dropped out of university, you don't have a job, you're always whining about being broke. You're risking your life for nothing. Here you've got everything, a home, a car... We can go to Moscow together if you want."

"She's trying to bribe me," thought Özgür. "She's afraid to take the trip by herself."

"I'm coming back," she said.

"When? If you come before January..."

She interrupted her mother. She was now talking with a mechanical device, the old battered plastic object that she held in her sweaty palm.

"I'm coming back. As soon as I settle accounts with Rio. If I run away now I'll be its prisoner forever. Do you understand, Mother?"

Silence...

"This city's killing me, Mom, every day, every minute, every opportunity, in every way, it's killing me. Slowly, insidiously... Down deep... It's taking away everything I have, right out of my hands. I'm surrounded, besieged, outside and in. I have to write Rio. I don't really think I can explain..."

"I can't hear you. It's so noisy over there. Those fireworks again! I was telling some friends about it the other day. About the favollos in Rio... They're called favollos, right? About how every Sunday they let off all those fireworks so the buyers know that the week's supply of cocaine has arrived... About how the whole city lights up with fireworks... Nobody believed me. They don't know

Rio so they asked me, naively, why the police didn't do anything about it."

"What FIREWORKS, Mom? What FIREWORKS?"

Her rage unleashed itself, rushing forth at full gallop. Straight into the jungle, full of insurmountable, thorny bushes.

"Don't you hear the machine guns? Those aren't fireworks, they're MACHINE GUNS! For God's sake, can't you even tell the sound of gunfire from fireworks?"

When, after a long, sorrowful sigh, her mother began to speak once again, her voice was coated by a thin layer of ice. A northern wind blowing in from a snow-covered Istanbul...

"What's going on over there? More military operations again? Look dear, you're making me sick with worry. You just up and left, just like that. Turned your back on all of us... Are you in touch with your father?"

"He hasn't called since September."

"He's mad at you for dropping out of school. All that studying just so you can throw it all away and loaf around! He doesn't understand what you're doing. But then, he always has been an insensitive ass."

For some reason, Özgür felt the need to stand up for her father.

"But he did send a suitcase full of clothes. And some Turkish delight!"

Of course, she didn't say that the clothes were too heavy and conservative for Rio. And she didn't blame her father for not having noticed all these years that she never, ever ate Turkish delight.

"He sent me Turkish delight—*lokum. Lo-kum...*"

She felt like she was rolling a big, sugar coated piece of *lokum* around in her mouth, sucking on it gently. There was something funny about the way those letters "O," "K," and "U" came together.

She let out a giggle.

"*Lo-kum*. Mint, rose, lemon, Antep pistachio…"

"What's wrong with you? Are you crying?"

She could hardly speak.

"No, I'm laughing. It's funny, isn't it? That word, *lo-kum*?"

Burst of laughter, bubbles jetting to the surface of a boiling swamp…

"Look, your nerves are all a wreck now. And I don't like the sound of that gunfire one bit."

"Oh now, why do you say that? I thoroughly enjoy it. I mean, Brazil's famous for its armed clashes, like Turkey's famous for its *lokum*. Don't you pay any mind to all that talk about carnivals and soccer…"

She began to laugh again. Inside she was telling herself that she needed to put a stop to this and regain her composure. She was about to puke.

"Anyway, I should go now. Do you need anything?"

This was the question she disliked most of all. She almost screamed, "Yes, I need a lot of things!" If only she could stop laughing… "Most of all someone who asks me what I need." She didn't respond.

"Okay, then. Bye…"

"Mom, wait. Are you going to call next week?"

"I doubt it. Maybe when I get back from Moscow. Okay dear, I miss you so much you know. Take care now."

"Mom, wait a second!"

There was a long, very long silence.

"Yes?"

"Mom, please, please don't leave me. Talk a little more," she thought to herself. Instead, she giggled.

"Okay then, God willing I'll see you in Moscow in January. Goodbye."

"*Hoshçakal*. Goodbye mom."

She held onto the phone as if it were a dead bird and continued listening to that expansive silence that is so much more meaningful, so much more agonizing than words. It was as if she'd gone deaf. The word "*HOS-ÇA-KAL*" ricocheted in her brain, like a prisoner pacing back and forth in her cell. The tak tak rhythm of Turkish's crisp, evenly paced syllables in military march... Unlike Rio Portuguese, which was reminiscent of a brook flowing hopscotch over pebbles, Turkish announced its meaning without any dilly-dallying or attempted seduction. The modern day fairytale known as communication had disintegrated, dropping flake by flake from the telephone wires, like the powdered sugar on *lokum*. She felt a chill within as she went to heat the teapot on the stove.

Seized by a sudden and irresistible urge, she sat down at the table, not even waiting for the water to boil. She titled a brand new, untouched page: "HARBORLESS VOYAGER." She wrote non-stop for several minutes, hardly even pausing to breathe. The unpunctuated run-ons of a writer lacking even the resolve to complete a sentence...

She wrote until that impulse that transformed her pen into a pair of shoes dancing by themselves on the stage of a famous musical had expired. She began to scratch the large cherry-sized mosquito bite on her elbow. First gently with her pen, then swirling the tip of her finger around the bump of it... But rather than subsiding, the itch gradually grew more and more intense until it was nearly unbearable. She angrily pressed her dirty, long fingernails into the very center of the red bulge and, with the rancor of a farmer driving his pitchfork into the cracked earth, ripped at her skin until a thin trail of blood oozed its way down to her wrist. The burning had finally subsided.

She reached for her pack of cigarettes once she heard the

teapot start to moan. There it was, another stroke of bad luck, another disaster to top off an already miserable day! She had only three cigarettes left. She began violently rummaging through the mess upon her table, as if her life depended upon it, searching for a spare pack. She had decorated the mahogany table, a reflection of Prof. Botelho's aspirations to nobility, with the cheapest, most common of objects lacking even a shred of distinction. A true spectacle of squalor consisting of a twelve-dollar "made in Paraguay" tape player, dusty cassette tapes collapsed in heaps like soldiers, bandages dangling from their wounded bodies, warped, steam-stained teaspoons, tin cans full of cigarette ashes, used band-aids, salt shakers that had failed to stand up to the humidity of the tropics for even three weeks, screws, nails, clothespins, batteries, pill bottles... Papers of every length and breadth: newspapers, magazines, cinema programs, tickets, posters, user's guides, worn sketch books, old photos as sorrowful as ships put on the stocks, unanswered letters from people whose very existence she now doubted... The pistachio green notebook containing *The City in Crimson Cloak*... Pens, ubiquitous, strewn everywhere... Seashells... Pincers, screwdriver, colander, can opener; tools and implements small and puny, yet of vital importance in the home of a bachelor... In more experienced hands this meager minimum-wage-working proletariat of featureless, unaffected objects would have mutinied against Özgür at every opportunity, putting up a merciless fight for its freedom. It was no use; there were no cigarettes to be found in this rat's nest! Three cigarettes at one cigarette every ten minutes; that meant that in less than half an hour she would have to go outside and look for an open kiosk in Santa Teresa, where the conflict raged on.

World-weary, she collapsed onto a chair, but only after having gotten a fresh cup of tea of course; she picked at her mosquito bites as she looked over the house, like a young woman searching for clues about the boy into whose bedroom she had entered for the first time. A kind of writing exercise...

She was a veteran migrant who had long ago learned that all of one's "indispensables" could fit into a single bag, that the rest could be thrown to the wind. She got absolutely no satisfaction out of claiming places and things as her own, or making them into reflections of her personality. In this house, pervaded by the rotting odor of the tropics, there was not a single non-functional thing, not a single item intended to appease the aesthetic senses. Like a vase, curios, flowers. Just as she had hated babies as a child, as an adult she avoided what she described as "feminine" items like the plague. She was so broke that she had no television, no washing machine, no chandelier, no mirror, no carpet, not even curtains. By means of a new technology that she had developed, she used the cornices to hang her laundry. She resorted to this because hanging laundry on the balcony was included in the twelve articles of prohibited acts typed out on a typewriter by Prof. Botelho himself. Her clothes, which because of the humidity never dried regardless of the temperature, and which grew dirty once again before she even had a chance to take them down, were quickly disintegrating, rebelling at the seams. But then nothing could stand the humidity of the tropics for long. Fruit spoiled in a few hours time, milk went bad, the soles of shoes came unhinged in a month, clothing grew moldy in the wardrobe, books, falling victim to the attacks of all kinds of fungi and bacteria, wilted away.

She ran her eyes over the books on the aluminum shelves as if to bid farewell. Fifty carefully selected Turkish books—she'd calculated one book per week, thinking that she would be here for one year—second-hand English novels; the only Portuguese book she owned, which she had bought because of the Nazım Hikmet poem it contained on the first page; Boal's prison diary...

The bloody-eyed, bloody-toothed snake-man, an Indian god that Roberto had brought from Amazonia, had turned his back to Tolstoy and was glaring at Özgür with eyes full of spite at having been plucked from the rainforest. In the corner stood her sullen, bulky suitcase, like a boxer of past glory who has not been inquired after for some time...

"This house is just a shelter for me," she thought. "Where I really live is a spiritual place that needs no ornamentation." Months ago she had changed her mind, deciding against her spy-like bound-to-secrecy attitude, and, like a cancer patient trying to add a friendly flair to her hospital room, had hung upon the wall something of sentimental value to her—a ballet poster. Yet in less than a month's time, one day when she wasn't at home, Prof. Botelho had come by to check the apartment; he had ripped the poster from the wall and tossed it onto the table, which he treated as a trash can, and left Özgür a note advising her to review the "list of prohibitions." (So it seems that Prof. Botelho did not trust his renters' taste and thus preferred to maintain a monopoly upon the right to decorate the walls.)

It was a dirt cheap, black and white poster made of ultra thin cardboard; it was so poorly printed that the dancers' facial features dissipated like Arabic letters dissolving in water. It contained the name of neither the photographer nor the ballet, but she recognized the latter immediately: Orpheus. Balanchine's Orpheus. Passion, rebellion, and desperation transformed into sculpture, becoming concrete in the perfected motion of two people... Eternity captured in a single motion, within a single moment... Humankind's fleeting, desperate, absolute victory over death...

She could imagine it right there before her very eyes: Together with his pure-blood German Shepherd Oscar in tow, and the even more devoted, pure-blood Rio mulatto housekeeper, her landlord

*marches in with all the pomp of a Roman warlord and has a look
around the living room; all the mosquitoes make him feel queasy
and so he covers his nose with a handkerchief to carefully inspect
the books and flip through their pages; he chooses a work of Marcus
Aurelius; with the tips of his noble fingers he rips the poster off the
wall and disposes of it.*

*Ultimately, by purifying her home of symbols and myths, and
destroying the sole projection of her soul that it contained, he had
taught her a lesson: All mirrors are empty in the city of vampires. In
the face of so much murder, torture, and death, he had shown her the
credulousness of seeking refuge in art, and in so doing had indicated
the empty walls. Those matte, whitish walls, their plaster swollen
and cracked, their surface covered in spiderwebs, rivulets of the blood
of dead mosquitoes, and stains shaped like humongous tears...*

Months later as she read what she had written, Özgür recalled a
coincidence that had up until that moment completely escaped
her mind—that *Black Orpheus* was the first film she had ever seen
that had to do with Rio. A musician hailing from the *favelas*, Black
Orpheus goes after Eurydice, making a journey in the Rio carnival, where mass hysteria, death, and chaos prevail; with his guitar,
which is able to open locked doors, he descends into the depths
of the Land of the Dead and reunites with his lover in a ritual of
the African religion, *Candomblé*. But at the very moment he has
defeated death, he opens his eyes, which he was supposed to keep
closed throughout the ceremony. Too early, like every Orpheus in
history... Only the guitar of Black Orpheus, a man fated to perish
in a *favela*, would remain.

Özgür had lit up her last cigarette and was staring into the
white walls. She felt as if rodents were gnawing at her heart. She
was angry at herself for having used up the telephone conversation she'd been awaiting for so long like that, and for not having

picked up around the house that Sunday, and for never managing to have a spare pack of cigarettes around. "Point Zero" was marching in place. "I haven't really lost all hope as long as I can still write," she thought. "But then *The City in Crimson Cloak* isn't exactly a text to be read with Chopin's nocturnes spinning on the record player, and it can't possibly be so; because where I write, it is the sound of gunshots that plays in the background."

Her eyes lingered upon the pen hanging from her fingers like a pack animal that's been worked to death. Then she wrote her name in huge letters in the center of an empty page: ÖZGÜR (FREE). She'd always hated her name, like she'd hated all blatantly obvious symbols. There probably couldn't be a more absurd, more ironic name than hers; it made one an object of ridicule in one's own eyes. For several minutes, the amount of time it took to smoke one cigarette, she drew, filling the inside of the "Ö". Four leaf clovers, skulls, treble clefs, infinity symbols...

Suddenly she sat bolt upright in her seat. From the pile upon the couch she chose a blouse, which was black and therefore concealed any tea stains, and a pair of jeans ripped at the knees. She didn't have the money to buy a new pair of jeans. She'd tried to patch this pair up but failed, and so she ended up having to live with the ever gaping rips, assuming the attire of a punk while standing at the threshold of thirty. She put a ten-*real* banknote in her wallet. She complacently noted that all together she had fifteen *reais* to see her through until Tuesday. She loaded a few lighters, pens, her sunscreen, wristwatch, telephone book, and keys into a bag the size of a small suitcase. And the good luck necklace of seashells, which had proven useless on numerous occasions, and her green notebook...

She always carried her novel with her, like an amulet, and whenever she wanted to retreat to her inner world, she would write, regardless of where she was. On the bus, at a kiosk, on the beach... The gunshots had stopped, and tranquility reigned for the time being. She hid the last bit of cocaine, which she'd concealed in the pages of *Hopscotch*, and her pocket mirror in the secret compartment of her bag. She knelt in front of the door and prayed that she make it through this journey in one piece. When she was seventeen years old she'd jumped up in religion class one day and declared that she was an atheist; all the other students glared at her like they wanted to skin her alive. But now here she was, unable to make the slightest move in Rio without first imploring the very same gods that she had denied her entire life to keep her safe.

"FIREWORKS DAY! Oh, how naïve I was back then." Originally she had attributed the fireworks that soared into the sky from some six hundred *favelas* every Sunday to the Brazilians' love of life, and she had been in awe of this exuberant people. It was only months later that she learned that the fake shooting stars announced the arrival of the latest batch of cocaine. "I wonder what it was that I lost that day—the day that I figured out what that 'shiny labyrinth' in the sky really was? My innocence? No, now, come on, nothing that could fit into such a bulky, insufferable word as that."

A TRAVELER
IN
THE STREETS OF RIO II

A traveler aimlessly wandering the streets of Rio, having taken refuge in her own self like a snail retreats into its shell, fearing the imminent pistol at her temple, her mouth like sandpaper, taking tremulous steps, large circles of sweat at her armpits... The horizon was limited by her vision, and she had nothing she could trust except for her own weary eyes.

The jungle, which had been the single, unconditional ruler of these lands not so long ago, only three centuries or so, was still there; it made its voice heard through the iron bars surrounding the huge apartment building. On every bit of these lands upon which the European had set foot, bearing his bloody cross—and sword, fever, torture, tuberculosis, syphilis—he had been defeated by the tropics. The White Man, who could not endure the jungle, the chaos, the unknown, and who sought to solve, resolve, and rule everything in which he meddled, was dragged into cannibalism, into insanity, on these lands. The tropical humidity worked its way into the marrow of his bones, and his moral fabric disintegrated under the sun and in the rain. The God who abandoned his very own son on the cross, and the one who discovered the rifle, failed to defeat African Eros, and so he put him up for sale, sullied him, and turned him into a crime. The rhythms of the Candomblé fused with hymns, lamentations, and the crack of whips.

In this city, which lies directly above the Tropic of Capricorn, all the possibilities of humankind are there before your very eyes, as if they are being offered up to a visitor from another planet... The black-whites, Indian-whites, Indian-black mulattos, Japanese, Indian, Russian, German, and the Swiss—who established colonies on every hill that even faintly resembled the Alps... Os Turcos, as the Syrian Arabs who brought desert melodies and içliköfte—meatballs fried in a cracked wheat coat—to Latin America are called... The dark Nordestinos (Northeasterners) through whose gullets pass nothing but coffee and cassava root, and who migrated from the sertões —wastelands—where feudalism persists to this day... The Bahiano, covered in the bloody scars of forty generations of slavery... The Amazon natives, who have the most impenetrable eyes in the world... And all other possible combinations... Blacks with indigo blue eyes, Indians with straw blonde hair, Japanese with African lips, Arabs with Kalmyk foreheads... Every color and tone possible to the skin of humankind... The color of cinnamon, the earth, bronze, milk, coffee, honey, chocolate...

The dizzying anarchism of the body... Bodies that have never learned of mystery, that have never known the thousand and one prisons of morality, thick sweaters, boots... Always fresh and lively, naked, stripped of myth... God bestowed unto these lands an endless summer, an endless youth. The colorful skirts of women billowing in the wind, the marijuana smoke enveloping the beaches, rhythms rising from scorching sidewalks to wrap themselves around hips, desire throwing itself off of cliffs like a rapacious bird... A city capable of breathing in the steam of sexuality: Rio de Janeiro. Always naked, yet always masked... Always sated, yet always ravenous...

THE MADMAN
OF
SANTA TERESA

Beyond a certain point there is no return.
This point must be reached.
—Kafka

At first, that indispensable condition of the vagrant life, penury, entered her life ever so quietly; like an insidious tumor that undergoes metastasis and then overtakes the entire body, it captured her suddenly, utterly, and completely. When she got fired from her job at the university, she hoped to work as a teacher at any one of the hundreds of English schools located throughout the city. But as it turned out, things did not go as planned. All of the good jobs had already been taken by American summer adventurers or vulture-like professionals who had dedicated their lives to English language teaching. Nobody trusted the oddly-named woman from a country that nobody could identify on a map. Throughout the month of January and its forty-degrees-in-the-shade weather, she had jumped onto buses packed full of people, the air heavy with human odor, incessantly en route, traveling from one neighborhood to the next, from morning until evening, writing various c.v.'s amongst the swooning passengers. She'd had interviews with a series of ever-so-chic, ever-so-haughty directors. They were young professionals, in love with their business cards, their chins held high as if to show off their Adam's apples, who believed teaching English to be the most important job in the world—and so too, undoubtedly, was everything else they did. What with her ragged purse, worn-out shoes, and hair that hadn't been touched by scissors for months, they had the pale woman sitting across from them pegged in a split second. And then there was the one language school that she managed to get hired by after much strenuous effort, only to swiftly get the boot because she refused to coddle the students and because of her persistent, know-it-all university professor attitude. And so, after shedding much blood, sweat, and tears, she got a few private students, most of them engineers who were lonely and therefore depressed, and who had developed an incestuous relationship with their computers; their eagerness to learn English, however, would be quickly extinguished as soon as she turned down their dinner invitations. And so gradually Özgür ended up having to cut back more and more. She could no longer even consider buying new clothes, or going to the barber or dentist or out to eat; abashedly she bargained with vendors at the local bazaars, she read the newspaper only one day a week, and she only attended shows and concerts that were free. The polar opposite of the classic stories of immigrants who gradually grew fat with wealth in the New World, her journey got started in the city's darling neighborhood, Copacabana; plain, "middle class"; she'd mapped out her route along the Botafogo and Flamengo gulfs, with their abundant churches, hospitals, and supermarkets, from the shores inland, straight into the heart of the city. From the white-skinned, touristy, air-conditioned Rio of appearances to the real Rio, mulatto, hushed-up, and hellish... From the Rio that gobbled up victories with an insatiable appetite, to the Rio that didn't even realize it was a constant loser...

Japanese cuisine was replaced first by buttery donuts eaten standing up, then later by *nanemolla*, and finally, once her "petit-bourgeois" stomach revolted, stark hunger. Milk coffee replaced freshly squeezed Amazonian fruit juices, and her Parliaments, the cigarette of career women, were replaced by L.M.'s, the cigarette of cashiers. She didn't even have enough money any more to buy FREE, the academicians' choice, with which, in a way, she shared a name. Counting her pennies was just too much for her; she was unable to deal with that common, simple, banal state suffered by nine-tenths of the world's population, that malady known as "poverty." Unfortunately, that particular intellectual attitude which doesn't personalize the issue, and which considers itself above the physical world, failed to sustain her ego. Out of the blue she had begun going through her old jewelry and wearing scarves, hats, huge wooden bracelets. Like the Africans say, "Pretentiousness becomes the hungry"... Whenever her money was about to run out, she would spend it more lavishly, squandering it on small indulgences, caprices, and gifts to pamper her ego. She would, for example, buy peaches that were twelve dollars a kilo and savor them, letting their juices drip, licking her fingers. She would frequent cinemas and watch film after film in which silence reigned and the setting was always a cold climate, and sometimes she picked up all the English novels on a street peddler's cart. Then there were times when, with flushed face, she'd hand over the little remaining money she had to a street kid. Spending her money to "treat herself" was like signing a ceasefire with life. Perhaps it would allow her to drink pleasure in tiny sips, and pain in tiny glasses.

"Money's like a crutch. It helps you stand upright." Every single God-given day she recalled this sentence, which she'd heard years ago from a taxi driver in Istanbul, the wisdom of which she was able to comprehend only once in Rio. Every time she was trodden down, every time she buttered someone up, every time she humbled herself... Every time she disobeyed the most basic principles of the "well-bred"...

One Friday night, she was at a currency exchange office in Flamengo. She had only ten dollars left to last her the entire weekend. Because of the unfathomable bureaucracy of Brazil, and its paranoid security measures, there had been a mix-up with her money as it made its way from signature to signature, and from hand to hand. She had been given the money of some pre-teen kid, whom she could clearly tell was an apprentice from the overalls he was wearing. Exactly thirty-two reais and forty centavos. She stood motionless for several seconds; her cheeks were on fire; there was a drone in her ears. She had two long nights and two long days before her, and a heavy, rusty, decrepit con-science which, despite numerous stumbles, still functioned... She put the money in her pocket. As she dashed out of the office, she saw how the apprentice boy counted the money given to him and stood frozen in horror, and how he headed for the counter with a tearful expression on his face.

She wandered about the streets for a while, like a prison escapee. Then she dove into the first Italian restaurant she saw and spent all of her money—all of the apprentice boy's money, all of the thirty-two reais and forty centavos that had cost so much toil, on a single dinner. There are some things more indispensable than virtue. Like lemon in your tea, the Sunday newspaper, or Italian mozzarella...

This was perhaps the most heartfelt part of the novel. Because it was so profoundly personal, she had used a straightforward, frank, bare bones style. Yet writing failed to purify Özgür of this utterly shameful memory. The eyes of the young apprentice would emerge from the dark corridors of her memory, crawling like a giant octopus, and grab her from behind at the most unexpected moments.

She had gently closed her door and glided down the stairs like a ghost to avoid encountering the mulatto Indian *portador* (care-taker) of the White Villa, Romario. She was in no condition to lis-ten to the five-foot, dark-complected, meek caretaker abashedly remind her about the rent once again. The check she'd received for two months' work from the last school she worked at had bounced; for weeks she had failed to convince the bulldog-faced boss in his Al Capone garb—cigar, patent leather shoes, bowler hat—to pay in cash. Actually, it was Romario whom she wanted to save from what would be an embarrassing exchange for them both. After all, she was the only renter to whom the poor fellow had shown his newborn child.

At this hour of the day, the house was dead quiet; the residents of Villa Blanche, who were hardly to be seen ever since the fighting started, had all gone down to the beach or to the mountain villages. At this hour, Romario must have been asleep in his dank quarters, with his sixteen-year-old girlfriend and two-and-a-half month-old baby. Prof. Botelho's pride and joy, the pure-blood German Shepherd *Guarda* (Guard), had vainly sought shade on the terrace, which gleamed like a mirror under the sun, before finally collapsing next to the low wall. Romario took out his persistent frustrations towards the White Man upon this defenseless animal; he'd leave it sitting out there all day on that hellish terrace, completely deprived of food or water. But then Özgür was the only one who was ever at all affectionate towards the poor animal.

She was in luck today. She had silently opened the triple-locked garden gate and managed to slip out without running into a single soul. It was Sunday evening, the time when she made her weekly trip to the small kiosk at the top of the hill, the only nearby place where she could buy cigarettes. The heat attacked her like an ana-conda, wrapping itself around her throat. It couldn't have been more than thirty-six or thirty-seven degrees; with her two years of experience, she could now tell from the sweat that instantly gushed out of her pores when the temperature was above body temperature. A common, warm summer day for Rio! But still she constantly felt as if she were standing right in front of a Turkish *döner* stand, meat spinning on a spit before the flame; no matter which way she turned, she felt the heat...

With their rose-colored, stereotypical phrases, tourist hand-books described Santa Teresa as "the center of Bohemian life," and recommended it only for the adventurous, or those traveling on a "shoestring budget." They recommended the hundred-year-old tramway that huffed and puffed its way up the stone-paved sidewalks, and a bar named "Sobrenatural"; they also strictly advised you not to wear a wristwatch, gold jewelry, or any jewelry resembling gold. An international scandal had broken out about two months earlier when a Japanese businessman, struggling to fend off an attempted robbery, fell off the tramway to his death (and during Brazilian–Japanese Friendship Week no less!), and all tramway rides were terminated. Thus was Özgür rescued from the vibrations that turned houses into convulsing malaria victims once every half hour, and those screeching brakes that sounded like the cry of a huge, metallic bird being strangled. Unfortunately, buses were now the sole form of transportation, for no taxi driver dared enter Santa Teresa, a place famous for its car robberies. Those godforsaken Santa Teresa buses, crammed full of people like sardines in a tin, their rates determined by their inevitably high-as-a-kite drivers... And as for the midnight bus! Whenever it slowly approached the bus stop, without a care in the world and at least twenty minutes late, there would be a burst of commotion in all the bars as the booze guzzling Santa Teresa crowd made a dash for the door, with their last beers or *cachaças*—a kind of rum—in hand. It would take another twenty minutes for the drove of eighty people, nearly all of them inebriated, to fill the bus, and no tickets would be issued, thanks to the unrecorded agreement between the battle-scarred ticket salesman and the neighborhood residents. Each person would hand over some money according to his means, keeping the driver's share in mind. Whatever they felt like giving... The bus, weighed down like an eight-months-pregnant woman, grumbled, occasionally coughed, and hiccupped its way up the steep hill. Each time it stopped and set off again, the boundaries between bodies would become clouded beyond recognition. The voice of a stone drunk negro would emerge from the back rows and break out in a samba; other voices, at first just a couple, then the whole crowd, would join in; the sound of a drum would step in to accompany the song; finally, the whole scene would spin out of control when the old ticket taker would turn the ticket box upside down and begin to keep rhythm. A midnight *festa* spontaneously born! Despite the fact that most of the passengers were drunkards, thieves, extortionists, or drug dealers from the *favelas*, not once had there ever been an incident of even pickpocketing, let alone armed robbery, on the midnight bus. A temporary fairytale of fraternity and equality, with pumpkins turning into coaches, and frogs into handsome princes, in bloody-handed Rio...

Santa Teresa was the sole hill in the city not yet overrun by the *favelas*; and it was also the sole neighborhood that belonged to artists, especially black artists. A rescued zone for musicians, dancers, painters, and artisans of everything from carving to perfume, rescued from the pinch of squalor thanks to their skills... Carnival kicks off here a day before its official opening; this is the only place where the birthdays of Nelson Mandela and of legendary resistance leader Zumbi, who founded the first black republic in history, are celebrated. Master interpreters of the samba, that "child of pain and father of happiness," play in the makeshift bars of Santa Teresa. (Those tourists with balls enough to enter the "black clubs" after dark are hard pressed to believe that those guys with their rotten teeth and ragtag clothes are musicians, men whose names had made it all the way to the northern hemisphere emblazoned on record covers.) With their wooden stools and rickety tables, pools of urine and long lines in front of faucetless restrooms, these bars, which served *cachaça* and beer on tap only, were always packed; and that darling of the middle class, the hollow, sugar-coated bossa-nova, was definitely not part of the repertoire. All the customers, except for the gringos, would accompany the musicians, keeping rhythm with drums, marimbas, and matchboxes, singing at the tops of their lungs and dancing, as the *samba* turned into *pagode*, the *pagode* into *maracute*, and the *maracute* into pure African rhythms.

In Santa Teresa, land of the perpetual carnival, there also lived a minority composed of ambassadors, politicians, mafia godfathers who wanted to stay out of public view, and former police chiefs who'd feathered their nests; these people lived in high-walled villas with their guards and Dobermans and never showed their faces on the streets. Özgür's landlord Prof. Botelho belonged to this caste, as did the gangsters who had carried out the greatest train robbery in English history before making their escape to Brazil...

Next to the Blue Mansion—one of those villas surrounded by electrical fences and glass shards—was Özgür's "Point Istanbul." At every stop in the course of her migrant life, from ocean shore towns to Alpine cities of Central Europe, at every harbor in which she had ever taken refuge, she had either found or created a Point Istanbul for herself. Places which, given the right perspective, the right light, and undoubtedly the right mood, resembled Istanbul... With its beaches separated by soaring cliffs, its sinuous coves that intertwine like the streams of the Amazon, its savage rocks ripping into the horizon, and its jungle like a boundless fishing net cast over the city, Rio was certainly nothing like Istanbul. It had a seductive beauty, one that was fond of extremes, contradictions, and imprudence; it pounced upon her, cruelly, inebriated her, took her firmly in its jaws. It had an eerie charm about it, like an African mask, while the city of her birth and childhood was like an antique silver bracelet, inlaid with amethysts, subdued, elegant, proud, tight-lipped, languid... But just here, only at this spot, which she reached by walking past the kiosk next to the tramway stop, taking care to avoid getting too close to the walls of the Blue

Mansion, Rio, a city that revels in the game of trickery, would remove its tropical mask and don the garb that Özgür wanted to see. The Atlantic Ocean, galloping towards the city at full speed, its mane billowing behind it, would pause suddenly in the mouth of the Guanabara Gulf, calm its waves which echoed eternity, and abdicate its vast throne. There, it would turn into a pale, coy, moss green inland lake; like a cat's tongue it would gently nudge its way into the humble, gently sloping hills of Niteroi. The Golden Horn as viewed from Pierre Loti...

Özgür came here every day she could muster the strength to leave her apartment; she'd stand straight and motionless amongst the wooden benches where all the homeless, the drunkards, and the cokeheads crashed, and wait for a breeze from the ocean to sweep her into the past. And usually the breeze would come, but in the form of a desert storm. It would fill her eyes with sand, raining down tiny molecules of volatile memories that scatter like sawdust, flickering images from the life that had quickly sunk into the depths of her memory, like a ship filling with water. Relevant or irrelevant, timely or untimely, tight-fisted, overseas memories... Memories that run out of breath all too soon, unable to transport her across those boundless waters separating her from her past... A scent, a sound, a boat horn, a pomegranate-colored sunset... Swift, smooth sailing into her childhood, and then, always, a locked door... Birds, unable to take flight though they flap their wings with all their might, would besiege her memory: only some stirring on the surface and a slight—not too much, not enough to hurt—melancholy... At such moments, Özgür felt the desire to write... Her past assumed a face only after she'd traced over its faded lines once again.

Yet beneath the commandeering, heavy-handed sky of the tropics, sometimes even "memory" seemed like a concept concocted by men of letters. Just a word. A skin containing no

soul, no essence... The most reliable refuge in the face of reality...
Özgür was now able to exist in a two-dimensional universe made
of words. In a universe in which death was reduced to the series
of letters: "D," "E," "A," "T," "H."...

Today was really her lucky day, for the wooden benches were
empty. Her mind at peace, she took her notebook, with its design
of green leaves, out of her purse. On the back cover of the notebook was written, "*Proteja a Natureza! A extinção é para sempre:*"
"Protect Nature! Extinction is forever."

*Why on earth did I ever choose this city that is so viciously cruel to me?
This Rio de Janeiro, which conceals its sharp, pointy teeth behind its
carnival masks, and envelops my very self in its crimson cloak, woven
fiber for fiber of human pain...? There is only one thing for which we
abandon safe waters and cut off our roots. Only one thing, for which
Adam rejected immortality: THE UNKNOWN.*

*It was a long, long time ago. I clad myself in the armor of loneliness
and set out to sea. At this final stop I have come to understand that my
existence is only going in circles. Armed with two dull swords, hunched
beneath the weight of my rusty shields. Each time only changing orbit,
never drawing nearer to the center... It is neither desire nor courage
which drags me from adventure to adventure. Perhaps it is the wish to
flee, but not from my past, for my past flees with me. Like a pickpocket,
running at full speed, and shedding left and right all the money out of
the wallet he has stolen...*

*Each journey is a change of décor, that's all. The panel with the
silhouettes of mosques is taken backstage, and the golden yellow sun
takes its place. A few palm trees, flashy beaches, a universe brought
into being with a few strokes of the brush... Cheap décor, a few amateur extras, the leading actor already alienated from the drama in
which he plays. And the music? Right now, the samba.*

If the past has turned into a lost Atlantis, and the dark shadow of the city is cast over all thoughts of the future, then you are forced to take refuge in "the present." You have no other choice but to be hurled between the sea and the jungle, between the arms of whites and blacks, from one bodily hunger which is easily satisfied, but which creates a thirst worse than before, to the next. Cleave onto wet lips until every pore of your body gushes, rip apart mangoes with your bare hands and suck the sugar from your fingers, puff on cigarettes as if inhaling pure oxygen, and dance! Distance yourself another step from your very self with each beat of the drum. Don't forget! That music, that music which grabs you by the shoulders and draws you into the country of madness, is the final remnant of the Black Orpheus.

She approached the kiosk, which was the size of a newspaper stand and reminded her of a gift in blue wrapping paper that someone had forgotten and left behind. At that point, she could have died for some *guaraná* soda and a cigarette. (Suddenly she recalled a midday in August when she had walked towards a historical looking, touristy kiosk in Sultanahmet. How the sun had warmed her back, the dusty avenue, the sesame ring peddlers... The kiosk sold sandwiches of white cheese and olive paste. But she wasn't in Sultanahmet, she was in Beyazıt, at the entrance to the café where she smoked waterpipe. She was eighteen years old, a university student; nothing significant had happened yet that day.) The most wretched, that is, the most genuine, of Santa Teresa's drunkards were the clients of this kiosk, which sold alcohol, cigarettes, and Paraguayan cookies that hadn't been touched for who knew how many years. A clientele of the homeless, bus drivers, the self-made engineers of the small *favela* who made their living in car thievery, the *capoeira* dancers who put on shows using knives (a combination dance/fight art of African origin which is based on sudden attacks and withdrawals and in which opponents never touch one another)... A clientele that chose to drink standing up—that is, until they collapsed onto the ground... On those rare occasions when Özgür managed to wake up early, she saw how the place was covered in broken glass, and blood stains.

A barefoot, mulatto youth, eighteen or nineteen years old, lay sprawled out on the sidewalk, snoring. Flies buzzed about his scrawny head, which looked like a skull carelessly slipped into a leather case; his right leg was in a pool of urine, most likely his own. At his head stood a pure-blood Siberian Husky, howling and moaning in pain. Most street people had dogs, and not just any dogs, but breeds like Dobermans, German Shepherds, and Afghani Greyhounds, which was utterly incomprehensible to Özgür. Why would someone who couldn't even find enough to eat for himself risk his life to steal a pup and raise it with so much self-sacrifice? Was it the need for security, or the need for friendship? After barking hopelessly for several minutes—during which time it had scrutinized Özgür out of the corner of its eye and realized it could not expect any favors from her—the disgruntled dog lay down next to its owner, placed its head on his stomach and quickly fell to sleep. "Not even the most destitute of humans awaken as much compassion as a helpless animal," thought Özgür, "Instead, the former rouses only a forced feeling of pity, horror, and usually revulsion... Humans are so merciless towards their own kind."

Two *favelados*, their gazes dark, stood in front of the tiny kiosk window guarded by iron bars. They were leaning up against the counter, enjoying their cold beers. Özgür, who had long before learned to always be on the lookout, immediately sensed that the men were up to no good. Long t-shirts down to their hips, swank shoes, gold-plated watches... Maybe they were a couple of Commando Vermelho's gangsters, taking a break between battles. She rather pessimistically began contemplating how she could slip by them and make her way to the window. The Rio Logbook of Death was full of those who had worn the wrong expression at the wrong place and been riddled with bullets; but she was dying of thirst. Moreover, she was prepared to fight like a gladiator for even one single cigarette.

"*Um guaraná por favor e uns* L.M. Lights," she yelled from two meters away in the most determined, most forceful tone she could muster. If this had been a theater stage, her voice easily would have reached the back rows.

Like all counter workers in Rio, the Portuguese operator of this kiosk, who was going on seventy, would remain impervious to customers' requests, reaching a satisfying climax only after he had tormented the petitioner sufficiently and made him repeat his request at least three or four times. "You off your rocker? Late to hell?" Özgür had withstood plenty of injustice, insult, and swindling, but the blatant rudeness of counter workers still drove her crazy. She irascibly began scratching at the mosquito bite on her elbow, now a bloody wound.

"*Por favor, um guaraná bem gelado e uns* L.M. Lights" Utterly unruffled, the man continued putting away bottles. Özgür was livid. If she'd had a gun at that moment, she would have put a bullet straight through that callous prick's ribs!

"Hey buddy, aren't you going to give me a *guaraná*? I've been waiting here under the sun for a full ten minutes."

With rheumatic slowness the Portuguese man gradually uncurled his back. He looked Özgür over from head to toe. He had light yellow eyes, eyes like those of a dead fish; there was no boundary between the iris and the white of his eyes, just like water and olive oil in the same glass. The look they gave her was more that of dreaming that she had never existed than wishing to exterminate the person across from them. The Portuguese man had long ago lowered his blinds on life. "Professional pervert, fucking pedophile," thought Özgür.

"Wait a minute, *gringa*!" the man replied, squeezing as much contempt and insult as he possibly could into four words. The Portuguese just couldn't bring themselves to do the legwork on these lands that they'd exploited to the bone, to the very marrow, for centuries, and so they unloaded their resentment onto other foreigners. And so now the very thing she feared had come to pass; as soon as the two *favelado* heard the word *gringa*, they pricked their ears like a couple of police dogs, and started looking her over, making no effort to hide the heavy, dark, greasy look in their eyes as they did so. "She doesn't have a watch or any jewelry, her purse's ragged but made of quality leather, definitely from Argentina. The heels of her shoes are worn. Just like the knees of her pants... Obviously doesn't have a dime to her name. But her poverty is temporary; she's just taking a break amongst the lowlifes who never got the smooth start she inherited. We're born destined to suffer, but they, they only choose to do so later. She'll go back to her nest, return to the privileges she's so easily squandered, but only after she's given up on accepting the world under her own conditions, only after she's learned to salvage the situation with a few minor concessions. As for us, though, nobody's ever given us anything; and that's why we'll take what we want, every scrap we can get."

Özgür's sixth sense was now as sharp as that of an animal being preyed upon in the dark. She clearly read every letter of the hate spelled out in the deep well of the Portuguese man's eyes. Still, she approached him with a fury she could not rein in. In a motion both childish and masculine, a motion she had likely learned from John Wayne films, she shoved the bottles aside and firmly placed her elbows on the counter. She'd let him know that she had no intention of leaving until she got her *guaraná* and cigarettes. She was like a gambler laying out everything she had, and, like all true gamblers, what she really wanted was to lose.

"A *guaraná*," she said, pronouncing the words one by one. "Right now. And a pack of L.M.... L.M. Lights."

She felt the pencil-mustached mulatto to her right freeze as if he'd just been tossed into a pool of ice water. She turned towards him. His eyes rained missiles upon her. She'd made a grave mistake! The insolent *gringa* deserved to learn a real good lesson now. That goddamn Portuguese! If he'd just slip her the *guaraná* so she could make a run for it! Their eyes shot balls of fire at her... At that moment she concentrated upon one single thing: the bottle of beer that stood between them... If she could break it, but even if she did manage to break it, what would she do with it... she wasn't giving a thought to the man on her left. Just the next move! The asphalt beneath her feet had turned into sand, and she was sinking. She felt that bloodthirsty wave rising up from the depths of her soul. That lust-like feeling, a sense of death... So who would get to it first? The black hand that was used to the holster, or the white one that had her way with nothing but the pen? Seconds that clotted, scattering like mercury... Özgür was now looking at the world from a constricted perspective, the bottle of beer and the jugular throbbing like clockwork on the mulatto's neck... Like a couple about to start a waltz, the two opponents stood facing one another; motionless statues. They were going to do the same dance—but neither pitied the other. They were nothing but puppets bowing down to the city's diabolical will. Preposterous, pathetic, murderous puppets... The sound of three bullets from a pump gun rang out from the valley.

"Hey *gringa*. Everything all right?"

Özgür instantly released all the tension in her body, like a marathon runner out of breath. Her muscles had suddenly become devoid of all strength. She nearly collapsed. The word "*gringa*," the same word that had almost led to her death only moments before, restored her to her proper self. It was Eduardo, the nephew of the former Rio Police Chief. She was saved, for now. It took several minutes for her to recompose herself; her hands were shaking, her heartbeat reverberating in her ears. She was drenched in sweat. The dance of death remained incomplete, like a session of lovemaking interrupted halfway through; the body, having failed to reach orgasm, was trying to rid itself of the energy it had amassed—trembling, convulsions, trembling. She'd made it through another dalliance, another flirtation, another *capoeira* with the City in Crimson Cloak.

"Hi. I'm fine..." Then after a while, she repeated, stuttering, "I'm fine."

Santa Teresa's most likeable bum, Eduardo, had given the mansion at the end of Murtinho street, the sole inheritance he got when his father was obliterated by a grenade launched at his car, over to public service, donating it to the homeless, drunkards, cokeheads, renegades, and the down-and-out. He lived next to the *favela*, in a reed hut that he had built with his own hands and which was filled to the brim with plants of the Amazon, cacti, and orchids. Truth be told, he generally passed out and fell asleep on the sidewalk or in the last bar he visited each night. It was said that he was a talented painter, and an incorrigible cokehead. He was a vagrant through and through; an emotional, kind-hearted, endearing crackpot who had indefinitely postponed settling his score with life.

"*Bonjour, mademoiselle,*" said Eduardo with an exaggerated gesture, giving her a low, Japanese style bow. He was aware of neither the time nor the dance of death that had been performed in the blink of an eye just a moment earlier. "You're looking a little down this morning."

Eduardo's face had that gray hue that people get when they haven't eaten in a long time. His cheeks were sunken, his eyes bloodshot. A glob of snot hung out of his nose. Indication of a heavy dose of cocaine very recently inhaled... Despite his disintegrating, oil- and paint-stained clothing, his ragged sandals with his pitch black toes jutting out of them, and his head of hair matted like a bird's nest, Eduardo still bore signs of the social class that he had renounced. He did not, for example, smell like those who grew up on the street, and every day he got a smooth shave.

"*Bonjour, monsieur*," Özgür replied, trying not to look at the man's face. She wasn't easily put off by bodily fluids. Rio had accustomed her to festering wounds, gangrene, and both defecation and masturbation out in the open, but for some reason, mucus still repulsed her. She would have to drink her *guaraná*, for which she had almost sacrificed her life, there in front of that piece of snot.

"Would you like to buy a necklace?"

Eduardo always carried a small display table with him; he sold beads and baubles, semi-precious stones, and astrology books, as the mood suited him. Actually, rather than selling them, he more often handed them out, especially to girls he fancied. After all, he really couldn't care less about money anymore.

"I don't have any money for a necklace."

She wasn't aware that when she spoke Portuguese, her personality changed, and she became someone harsh, rigid, and blunt. She understood the language almost perfectly by now, but she had not yet achieved fluency in speaking. She could express herself in only the most direct manner.

"Then let me give one to you, as a gift. Choose one! Take all of them, if you want. Business sucks anyway. Because of the boom boom boom boom."

With an invisible gun he unleashed a series of bullets on the Santa Teresa Valley, and the kiosk. Özgür leaned her head slightly forward and noisily exhaled through her nose and puckered her lips. It was her attempt at a smile.

"Thank you, but no. I really don't want one."

Eduardo scrutinized the pale-faced, dejected-looking *gringa* from head to toe. The woman's face was calm, as if she'd just taken a hit of opium, but the numerous lines, like traces of waves on pebbles, gave her away; clearly she had had her fair share of quarrels with life, and gotten her fair share of roughing up. She had none of the lively, flirtatious manner, or flagrant sexuality of the Rio women about her. Hers was an undecorated, plain, mostly lost beauty... He'd watched her from afar in the bars of Santa Teresa. She was always alone, always sitting at a table in some secluded corner, chain-smoking and scribbling things on napkins. A half-living monument of sorrow, with no intention of infecting others with her unhappiness. Though she reeked of loneliness, she always rebuked the jackals that descended upon her, and under no condition did she ever let down her guard. He'd heard it said of her, who was rumored to be a Syrian author, "This woman is loneliness personified. A Middle Eastern goddess whose cult has disbanded, her temples covered in graffiti." Perhaps the inexplicable weakness he felt for the *gringa*, whom he actually didn't find to be all that attractive, was because of this sentence, which he just couldn't get out of his head; so far, he had showered her with gifts at every opportunity: Silver earrings, astrological maps, a pair of sandals. Özgür's ears weren't pierced, she couldn't care less about astrology, and she detested open-toed shoes. Still, she stored the gifts away carefully. Nobody except the tender-hearted, crazy Eduardo had given her anything in Brazil, though she'd already spent two birthdays there.

"The governor's in Santa Teresa. I read it in the newspaper. He's here to put an end to the fighting."

A naughty sparkle twinkled in Eduardo's iridescent eyes. A slightly protruding, heart-shaped dimple very becoming to his long face appeared on his chin.

"The governor and all those stiff suits... They're going to fuck up Santa Teresa. They're going to build a police station every half kilometer. They can kiss my ass. Here where this kiosk is, too."

"Really? But isn't this a historical site?"

"Here ya go dear, *guaraná* and L.M. Lights."

The old Portuguese man, whom not five minutes earlier she had dreamt of sending to Never Never Land with a single shot through the ribs, was finally handing over the desired goods. Özgür felt ashamed. The violence that had grown in her heart like a stalagmite ever since she'd begun to live in this city frequently took over the reins to her being. She had horrific, stomach- churning fantasies that she just couldn't reconcile with herself. Like holding a gun to the head of bus drivers, counter workers, her boss, and informing them in a cool, indifferent voice that if they didn't give her her salary or her coffee right away, she was going to pull the trigger.

"I, um... Thank you."

She found a five-*real* banknote without having to take her wallet out of her purse. She had turned her back to both the *favelados* and to Eduardo, and held her bag close to her body. Habits she'd picked up in the New World... When she approached the counter, she saw that the two mulattos were no longer paying her any attention but were deep in conversation, as if that *capoeira* of death of just a few minutes before had never actually happened. She was shaken by an awful feeling of doubt. Could it be that all of this—the beer bottle, the crimson cloak—was nothing but a fiction of her internally bleeding imagination? Maybe these men sipping on their Sunday beers were not out to get her. Why hadn't it occurred to her that their blood-chilling glances could just be out of curiosity, or sexual attraction? And to think that she had already written that very same scene herself. The protagonist of

the novel, still named just "Ö," a half-fictional "Özgür," almost
got into a scrap with two jailbirds at some decrepit place in Lapa
called "The New World," her life barely saved by mere coincidence.
"The violence within and the violence without... The boundary
stones separating the two are being dislodged one by one. Life
and writing stand opposite one another, like two ventriloquists
speaking from their bellies. Each constantly trying to drown out
the voice of the other. I'm no longer certain which it is that I hear.
This must be what madness is like."

She took a long, lustful gulp of *guaraná*. By the time she had
quenched her thirst, the bottle was nearly empty. She got a high
from the sugar that rushed to her brain. She licked her lips at
length as she ripped open the cellophane-wrapped pack of cigarettes.

"You do this?" she asked, indicating the charcoal drawing on
the display table.

It was the face of a negro, long as if it its cheeks were being
squeezed together, its cheekbones resembling those of a skeleton.
A callous, fragile, sorrowful narrative like a scabbed wound... He
looked like he'd just gotten out of prison. Özgür saw the same face
in that of the wide-eyed, downtrodden woman she sometimes
watched from behind dirty bus windows; but she was incapable
of feeling even the same pain for that woman as she did for this
portrait.

"Yes, *gringa*, I drew it. Or don't I look like an artist? All of Santa
Teresa knows that I'm an artist. And I'm an architect, too."

"Really? You made all of these? This kiosk, this square, Santa
Teresa?"

Having lit her first cigarette, she was now in a supremely good
mood. She could make all kinds of nonsensical chitchat for hours
standing there under the hot sun. Eduardo attributed the *gringa*'s
odd question to her limited Portuguese. He bowed his head, spit

onto the ground, and mumbled something or other. Maybe the woman just had a screw loose.

Suddenly Özgür felt that one of the countless puzzles of her memory had for no apparent reason been solved. That day, when she had eaten the olive paste and white cheese sandwich in Beyazıt, SOMETHING had happened. Something that had wounded her deeply... A conversation. In the courtyard where she'd smoked from a waterpipe...

"Do you speak English, Eduardo?"

"Very little. I love you, *gringa!*"

Özgür once again replied with the puckered face that she'd acquired in Rio, as substitute for a smile. It seemed that she'd heard this sentence in various languages and tones since her early childhood, and she was sick to death of it. She'd once been a beautiful woman, but she'd lost her beauty before she could learn how to use it properly.

"That really is very little."

"Come over to my place. I've got some high quality snow; we can have a little fun together."

"No thank you," replied Özgür, with the Old World politeness that she had retained, in full, throughout the two years she'd been in Brazil. She'd received numerous such invitations to go to bed; out of the blue, informal, unceremonious. Only on the first such occasion had she been shocked by it; while standing around eating pizza, a friend of a friend, whose name she couldn't recall, began caressing her neck and telling her that he was dying to make love to her, and she choked.

She grew silent when she sensed the change on Eduardo's face. She felt the eyes of a raptor upon her. Watching Eduardo's eyes grow suddenly serious, she then saw that the madman of Santa Teresa was standing right next to them. He must have slipped up unnoticed, from behind the kiosk, with the silent footsteps of a leopard. His blue, phosphorescent eyes were fixed upon Özgür. She was totally immobilized; in the presence of a madman she became dumbstruck, as if in the presence of a king, for she found the insane even more frightening, more elusive than the dead.

March marks the end of the long dry season in Rio. It's the month when the tropical rains begin, rains that persist for days, nights, weeks. A huge army clad in black suddenly spreads over the horizon; it approaches at a gallop, full speed, and attacks just like that, without warning. It descends upon the city like an abominable, inescapable fate, without even allowing time to pull down the shutters. A furious, savage, vengeful, insufferable, merciless downpour... The sky finally rebels, determined to eradicate all of this filth—the streets, the sky-scrapers, the blood, and the history—and turn the city into a river, drowning it in the ocean. To return these lands to their real owners, the jungle... To return to those beloved, pre-human days, when time did not yet flow... The drops burn like acid; they strip the color from objects, and the oldest recollections from memory. The floods, draping themselves over all, sending everything awash... The ocean, besieging the city with its awful, uproarious laughter; seagulls going mad amongst the spume... Gigantic waves breaking upon the docks whisk away, without prejudice, all that stands in their path. Palm trees, gar-bage, beach umbrellas, bicycles, drunkards, street people...

That night was her birthday. The lake at the heart of the city had flooded, and the water was waist high even on the main avenues. Telephones had been down for a week. Late one night, she'd come upon a table of people from the street theater. She was so distraught that she hadn't the strength to respond to even the most sincere of smiles. She'd been waiting for hours for the rain to stop. Her apartment was a stone's throw away, but she had no desire to venture outside, not with the huge pellets of rain coming down. Near dawn, when the musicians took a short break for an "alcohol boost," a goblin appeared at the bar entrance, a gigantic hirsute man with water running down his pants which were held up by a piece of twine. His heavy scent preceded him, settling upon everything like a thick fog. He was leaning against a column on his left arm, standing there like the sphinx, patiently scrutinizing everyone one by one. A merciless gaze impervious to illusion, fully cognizant of the true meaning of that thing called "the human soul"... He held an overwhelming sway of unknown origin over the group, each member of which was a puppet, the strings in his hands. Each time their gaze met, she felt herself shiver like a sign whose nails were being yanked out by a violent wind. The madman had eyes the likes of which she had never before seen in her life; cobalt blue, metallic, with an odd glint that almost seemed to emit a radiation with mass. Two stars twinkling on his face, absorbing the darkness; two super-novas on the verge of explosion. A chemical fire, both burning caustic and chilling, enveloped her conscience.

The goblin walked over to her, as if she were the last person on earth with whom he had not yet settled scores. He stood tall before her, like a proud plane tree. He was very, very tall; he had a nose like the beak of an eagle, and straight, raven black hair, like that of an Indian. And huge, black rings beneath his eyes... He was really very ugly, but even in his ugliness there was a kind of magnificence.

"Seus olhos *(Your eyes),*" the man said, *mumbling then a few indistinct words.*

She vaguely heard the theatrical acrobat Andre say, feeling no need to lower his voice, "Don't worry, gringa, he's harmless." *She was stunned into silence.*

"Meus olhos?" *(My eyes?) she stuttered in her poorly accented Portuguese.*

"Estrangeira?" *(Foreigner?)*

She gently nodded. The man broke into impeccable Oxford English.

"I said, your eyes are like no others."

She shuddered, as if trying to shake herself free of some heavy drug, and indicated the Spanish-Indian mulatto Tanja who was sitting next to them.

"Her eyes are more beautiful than mine."

"I didn't use the word 'beautiful.' I said they are incomparable."

Though she thought to ask him just what he meant by "incomparable," inside, she remained in a daze.

"The Human Dress, is forged Iron. The Human Form, a fiery Forge. The Human Face, a furnace seal'd."

At that moment, she felt the bell jar around her head rise. This was exactly what she'd been searching for for months: Someone who spoke his own language. Like someone dying of thirst in the middle of the ocean, that's what she'd been looking for. For the first time, she met the madman's glance with the same intensity, and said the final line:

"The Human Heart, its hungry Gorge."

The goblin's reaction was violent. He started into a long, complicated tirade. He spoke breathlessly; he was raining down words, sentences, verses, like bullets from a machine gun. A quotation from Macbeth, a famous line from Keats... Those were the only ones she recognized. She couldn't keep up with his thoughts, or keep track of his chain of associations. It was neither possible to join in on his delirium—and she wasn't even sure if that's what it was—nor to stop it.

Within a few minutes' time the bar owner, Arnaudo, came running over with two waiters, took hold of the man, who had just skipped from literature to philosophy and was talking about Locke, and grabbed him and dragged him out of the bar like a head of cattle. She was able to understand only a single sentence of their profanity-ridden argument.

"I want to talk with her, not with you, WITH HER! Just talk..."

The theater actors intervened to help send the madman packing without doing him too much damage. And thus did the gruesome miracle, the sole gift she had received on her birthday, disappear just like that. She felt awful, a fist of guilt clenching inside of her; and she took refuge in a cigarette. Andre had thrown his arm around her, with typical Brazilian indifference—they couldn't stand still without having their hands all over one another like lovebirds—and begun stroking her neck.

"You know that man, right?"

"No."

"Senhor de Oliveira."

The only thing she recognized was the word "oliveira"—olive grove.

"He was one of Brazil's leading painters in the 1980's. In fact, he's the man who introduced Brazilian art to Europe. He lived in England. The man's got culture, seriously."

She found herself stupefied once again, but not really surprised. A boring, ordinary, desolate evening had suddenly taken on profound meanings, signs, and mysteries. Like the bus drivers who transformed into ogans, kings of the world of spirits, in the Candomblé rituals.

"So why is he like that? Crazy? Crazy-like?"

"He got that way after he came back to Brazil. He's not crazy, I mean, not all the time. He lives in the Blue Mansion next to the kiosk. Actually, he's a very pleasant fella when he's got his head on straight. He's amazing. But then, as you've seen, sometimes the mood strikes him, and he just unleashes himself onto the streets."

"Does he still paint?"

"As far as I know, he quit. As soon as he got back to Brazil."

A heated discussion was now underway. How artists weren't given their due in the Third World, the demise of the most important values, etc. The street theater actors identified themselves with Oliveira and were trying to claim a piece of his genius—for it was unanimously agreed that he was a genius. Meanwhile, Arnaudo had come up to her and, wringing his hands, apologized; he said that the lunatic had never bothered anyone like that before, and so that's why he hadn't thought to take action earlier. Arnaudo, born and raised in Santa Teresa, did

*not know who Oliveira was. Ö. felt like she was drowning, and she
made a mad dash out of the bar, despite the rain. She ran to and fro,
the raindrops whipping against her face and trickling in beneath her
collar; hopelessly she sought Oliveira, the goblin who had disappeared
into the stormy darkness.*

They ran into one another again two months later. It was at her
Point Istanbul. Oliveira was wearing a black tuxedo; he looked
so elegant and smart that Özgür was able to recognize him only
from his eagle nose. Next to him was a woman drowning in jewelry and make-up. Clearly, she belonged to that social class which
comprised the main buyers of the art world. A haughty muse a
bit gone to seed... Oliveira did not respond to Özgür's persistent
glances; he definitely did not remember her. That odd, bewitch-
ing twinkle had disappeared from his eyes; the stars were extinguished, now nothing but dead celestial bodies.

Their paths had crossed several more times since their initial
encounter. On occasions when Oliveira was a street person, or
during those spells when the nameless street person shed his
Oliveira shell. Every time he had suddenly appeared at Özgür's
side and stood there, silently, motionless, enveloping her in a
tragic, blue light that transformed her into a skeleton. His eyes
were like phosphorescent leaves giving off the only light in a dark
jungle. He never spoke to her again, except for the one time he
said to her, "*Seus olhos.*" Every time, Özgür was overcome by an
uncontrollable sense of uneasiness and distanced herself from
him as quickly as she could.

But today, she was determined not to run away. She wanted
to talk with Oliveira, to get a response out of him, no matter
what the cost. It was too much; she had to tell someone what
was happening.

"Don't worry, he's harmless." It was Eduardo who broke the

silence. "He wouldn't hurt a flea. He doesn't even talk. He just stands there and looks."

Özgür considered telling him, "But he talked to ME," but then changed her mind.

"You remember me, don't you?" she said, addressing him in English. "You know, that night, last March, you recited that famous quatrain by William Blake. And the last line, I..."

She felt like a complete idiot. The goblin didn't even hear her. Just like Eduardo had said, he just stared, nothing more. Without seeing... His eyes were filled with an adoration bordering upon worship. "I must remind him of another woman. Maybe the woman who drove him insane," she thought.

"He can't understand you," Eduardo interjected. "He goes weeks without speaking, eating, drinking. I usually take him to my hut, clean him up a bit. You know, because he shits himself and stuff. You wouldn't believe it, but he used to be a very famous painter. In England..."

Özgür did not even hear his words. She was completely concentrated upon one thing, and one thing only, like a hunter. Actually, she didn't know what she was after. The word in the dark, the light reflecting off of the silence? Or some other awful miracle?

"It is a tale told by an idiot," she said slowly, assuming full responsibility for the words that she spoke, "full of sound and fury..." She wouldn't be able to say the last line without her eyes brimming with tears.

"Signifying... Signifying nothing..."

Oliveira's eyes suddenly gleamed like a sun setting within himself and a wave of pain washed over his face, a sculpture in granite.

"I really should take him to my hut. Otherwise he's bound to get blown away by some stray bullet."

"*Senhor de Oliveira...*" She was nearly begging him now. It was the courage of a poker player laying down his final trump card. A person could hardly be so far gone as to forget his own name.

"*Senhor de Oliveira*. There's something I want to ask you. I should ask, not why you no longer talk, but perhaps why you once did."

"   "
 ...

"*Senhor de Oliveira*, why don't you paint anymore? Or why did you once? Seeing as you would ultimately take refuge in silence...? What I'm really trying to understand is this: I can breathe now only when I sit in front of a blank piece of white paper—in a way, an empty, deaf wall to which I have nailed myself—and fill it with words. The words are empty. But still they fill my vacuous life. In fact, they overtake it, replace it. You understand me, right? I sense that you do."

Silence... Emptiness... Oliveira was obviously, clearly, simply not there. He was not present, not even in his own eyes. Özgür suddenly began to scream.

"For God's sake, what do you see in my eyes?"

From her lips had escaped the last question to which she was prepared to hear the answer. She froze, filled with the premonition of a horrible prophecy. Such as "*A MORTE!*"; the sentence of death in a language other than her mother tongue. But Oliveira was merciful, at least on the days when he took refuge in the streets. He returned to Özgür what she had given him: Emptiness. He didn't say a word. She calmly submitted when Eduardo grabbed her by the arm and began to drag her away.

"By the way, I thought you might want to know, his name is Eli," a voice said, in Portuguese.

"WHAT? WHAT DID YOU SAY?"

"His name is Eli," Eduardo repeated, nodding towards the madman. The man was completely devoid of will and spirit, and gave no reaction whatsoever. He did not even react to his own name... His eyes were still focused upon Özgür.

"*Eli, Eli, lama sabakhtani*?"

"Sorry, what? What is that? Arabic?"

"Something like that. It's Aramaic... The last words that Jesus spoke on the cross. 'Father, father, why hast thou forsaken me?'"

"That's all mumbo jumbo to me, sweetheart. I carry my gods here, inside. Well, see you later, lover. Kisses." The last word he spoke in English.

Özgür couldn't help but give him an agonized smile.

"Just be careful they don't escape. It's a wretched age we live in. The streets are much too dangerous! Kisses to you, too, Eduardo."

All of her courage, her strength, her desire to live had melted away like a candle. She was covered in sweat from head to toe. That insidious tremor settled onto the corner of her mouth once again. She felt the muddy gaze of the Portuguese man on her back. She turned around. The *favelados* were gone. She was overcome by an awful, ash-gray loneliness.

She lit a cigarette and began walking down the Santa Teresa hill. She couldn't stand to go back home and be alone with her addled inner world. With the echo of silence in her ears... She felt guilty. She'd tried to exploit Oliveira, prisoner to the luster of his own cocoon, and sought in his spectrum of light, which reached to the greatest extremes, a vibration for her own benefit. She had become much too dependent upon the word, whose sacredness had been declared in the Old Testament.

"For God's sake, what do you see in my eyes?"

What audacity! How could she have forgotten that in this city, all manner of "thoughts of the future" became but a fear of death from their very inception? The madman had taught her a momentous lesson and sentenced her to life instead of death. She stood, stunned by a razor sharp enlightenment—her cigarette had fallen

from her hand. The answer that she ran from—and chased after—in horror was not death. She had been afraid that Oliveira
would see the reflection of his own eyes. That he would sense the
presence of those same magnificent stars, of the diamond-tipped
arrow of insanity in her eyes... "I'm just hallucinating again. I remind him of another woman, that's all. A woman from his past, a
woman he renounced."

She recalled, as she bent over to pick up her cigarette, why the
day she had eaten the olive paste and white cheese sandwich in
front of the touristy kiosk in Beyazıt had not been an ordinary
day. She was eighteen years old, fresh back from her first vacation
in Bodrum, and she was meeting her lover. "I had this adventure,
so passionate, like the summer rain," the young man had said to
her. "I thought I'd fallen in love with someone else. But then I
understood that, really, it's you that I love."

A long forgotten first love, still smarting ten long years later...
But it seemed that even in the midst of that pain lay a kind of
happiness. Happiness at having been loved, once, by even a single
person in this whole wide world...

It was almost sundown; she decided to go down to Lapa and
lose herself in the city crowds. She walked towards her own private Rio, erect and rigid as a rock, full of acrid, forlorn defeat,
and brimming over with her own private pain. Her footsteps
were hard and determined, as if she were preparing for a terrible
battle; but her sorrowful shoulders belied her courage to be that
of a mere poser.

HARBORLESS VOYAGER

Voyagers, swept up and deposited upon this forsaken continent, so far from the focal point of civilization, by who knows which winds, undertows, countercurrents... Old Nazis, outlaws, international terrorists, fallen dictators, sailors, those who've traversed the ocean in quest of the specter of freedom... Those who journey all the way to the tropics, chasing a recollection of love that has ripened to perfection in the mind; those in search of "themselves," of lost Atlantises; those who believe music, dance, and passion to be the antidote to all existential pain... Those who leave behind not only their coats and boots, but their consciences, too, to pursue the dirt-cheap loins of children... Incurable romantics, their rooms adorned with Che posters, who head straight for the swamps, believing that there are no more ideals worth dying for in their own countries... Those who skip from one horizon to the next, always longing for the distant, farther, farthest continents... Those who escape to South America, the blank canvas upon which to paint all their dreams; South America, that knotted bundle of illusions, promises, and fairytales... And those who collapse down on their knees and lick the floor in the châteaus of their fantasy...

World migrants... Devil-may-care wanderers, night roamers, migratory birds... Those who walk alone on this great, infinite road... Those who always travel with one-way tickets, those who disappear without a trace, those who spend decades living out of a suitcase... Those who refuse to be tied down, to be grounded, to integrate, who cut their roots for the sake of a pair of wings incapable of carrying the weight of their bodies... Those with a fondness for deserted, rugged

paths, back streets, and the outer fringes of memory... Those who pre-
fer the dark wings to the bright stage... Those who eddy back and forth
between two imaginary harbors, one hidden in the past, the other in
the future... Harborless voyagers...

Letters which gradually become less and less frequent, and more
and more repetitive, three-penny postcards, trite words of separation
full of made-to-order smiles, photographs taken in poor lighting, gifts
light in terms of weight and value, obituaries full of spelling mistakes
squeezed into just three lines... "Our Consulate hereby announces the
death of T.M., citizen of the Turkish Republic and holder of passport
number 011-7143, on 4/24 in a horrendous traffic accident..."

AWAY

Heaven is a league beyond hell,
Hell a step past heaven.
—Iranian Proverb

The evening she bought her notebook with the "Protect the Environment! Extinction is Forever" cover, she had been released from the police station after eight hours of torture. She'd dashed into a pizza place in Catete; there, she drank glass after glass of papaya juice, cup after cup of coffee, and smoked nearly an entire pack of cigarettes; then she bought the thickest notebook she had ever seen in her life from a street peddler. However, days would pass before she would finally be able to write the following on the first page:

I swear to tell the truth, the whole truth, and nothing but the truth. That's the opening sentence for those in the witness chair, or at least it is in Hollywood courtrooms... But an author who starts off with these words should accept defeat by knock out from the get-go. Even if he only attempts to write of phenomena—phenomena that are plenty eager to speak for themselves—as soon as he begins to fill in the matrix before him, he has to make certain choices. What, whom, which one? He will see that different sequences of the same phenomena give birth to entirely different realities, like the innumerable hands of poker produced by a pack of 26. And he cannot contend to be objective in the choices that he makes. Prejudice, favoritism, a case or two of subterfuge, a little scheming, inevitably become part and parcel of the endeavor at hand; all of the fears, expectations, and feelings of worthlessness that he had recoiled from admitting will suddenly one day come to light and nibble away here and there at the power of observa-

tion of which he is so boastful. For no ego is small enough to face up to its own reality. And if he has been able to make it through this phase without losing his belief—in which case he should be congratulated for his pluck and idealism indeed—then, once he comprehends that he has to build, with his own hands, a bridge between words and phenomena, a bridge without a railing, and to accomplish everything by himself, from the choice of materials to the lighting, the humiliation will teach him a good, hard lesson. But the most horrific disappointment awaiting him comes at the end of countless days and nights spent between four walls, and which take place in an ocean of ashtrays and further deepen yet another crease on his forehead. And what emerges after so much effort, sacrifice, agonizing, and emotional turmoil is not at all the bridge he was hoping for; it is not a bridge to the outside world. As life continues flowing by, with all of its indifference and irreverence, he will find that he has managed to construct nothing more than a personal observation tower in the gruesome desert of reality. A brittle, moaning tower, full of the wind blowing in through its cracked wooden planks… In the end, everyone who takes up a pen must struggle with this question: How much reality CAN I STAND?

She didn't know when she'd decided to write *The City in Crimson Cloak*; in fact, she didn't even think that such a "decision" had been made. Like everything of determining character in life, it was the product of unexplainable accidents, encounters, and co-incidences. Born suddenly, like passion, it had caught Özgür unawares. Its head hung in sorrow, like that of an unwanted child.

In her first pain- and fear-filled months in Rio, her imagination writhed, like a mare that swells and swells but just cannot give birth. The transformation that she had labeled "Process: Destruction" was proceeding at an astoundingly swift pace. Everything decayed so quickly in the tropics, and revived just as swiftly. In a single night a jungle of weeds, thorny bushes, and poison ivy would sprout up, replacing felled trees. Chaos replaced order, pieces the whole, wild the domestic... Perfect proof of thermodynamics in this universe, which is said to be governed by the laws of physics...

She'd plunged into passion with the mettle of a novice, and the impudence of the parvenu... She'd tasted the belatedly discovered intoxication of skin in magical and common embraces. She'd been seduced by Latin names, resonating like guitar strings, always ending in a cotton soft "o"—Fernando, Roberto, Rodrigo—and each time, she had fallen madly in love. They had easily disposed of her with their empty promises. With a beautiful saying, a promise, a warm smile, a night of love that clotted her loneliness rather than extirpating it... (And always the same explanation: Please don't take it personally. This is Rio de Janeiro.) "I absolutely have to see you. Right away, tonight. I miss your scent so much. I'll call you at five." She'd heard these same sentences in various sequences and from various lips countless different times. She had only believed it once, the very first time she heard it. She'd walked out of the theater halfway through the film and rushed home as if by flying carpet in order to make it in time for that "enchanted" five o'clock. For hours, days, weeks, she sat by the telephone, unable to tear herself away. Like a mother who just can't believe her child is stillborn...

Because she couldn't deal with the long nights that extended before her like black tunnels, she clung to the human body, salve for the worst possible pains; she had docilely acquiesced to having her frail sexuality punted from one born samba dancer to the next. Of course she had come to the realization that she was nothing but a bimbo prop in their love stories; but she was so overwhelmed by loneliness that she was prepared to content herself with the wobbly, fragile breath of love present even in the most self-seeking relationships. Her power of imagination transformed insubstantial memories into fairytales; and her memory increasingly exaggerated the pleasure she had derived, and the role she had played. At the pinnacle of the art of self-delusion, she would embrace the telephone; as soon as she heard that saucy, obnoxious, insolent Rio "Oyyy!" sound on the answering machine, she'd hang up the receiver, in disgust.

This city had relinquished her, and she in turn had relinquished her self. Otherwise, she never could have offered up her body so easily and, unfortunately, in Rio's vocabulary of love, it was the body that had the last word.

The person she had spoken with on the telephone only an hour ago and agreed to meet here had stood her up, making her wait all alone for hours in the most dangerous part of Rio. The second salary check that her boss gave her, with a thousand and one apologies, had bounced; after taking three different buses at the break of dawn for a lesson, her student turned up missing; as she was returning home on an empty stomach, not yet having had breakfast, a street kid put a knife to her throat and demanded the money that remained in her bag. Her friends tried to tempt her lovers before her very own eyes, and what's more, expected gratitude for having shown her the fine points of seduction. The streets of Rio that she tried so hard to keep away from her inner world were much more than she could take. Gangrenous wounds, gunshots, and sexuality... Every step she took, another hungry child appeared at her side, leaving her to confront this question: Am I losing my humanity? Or is this what being human means?

The principles that she had developed, distilled through her experience, had been expended, cruelly consumed, and made a tool to various ends. The islets within the circle called "I" had escaped her one by one and formed independent satellites around her. The empty shell left behind meanwhile had been abandoned to destruction, decay, and the mercy of time, which doesn't play favorites.

At first she took refuge in her ancient friend, literature; she sought an author who could shed light upon the night that gradually deepened within her. An author who'd set foot upon wild lands, who'd had the blade of a knife pressed against her throat by a twelve year old—a mere child. Özgür now had two separate worlds. In the first world, woven of piano sonatas and Chekhov stories, that broad, deep ocean called life was depicted on a thin seashell, while the second belonged to deceptions of love, hit men, and the voracious jungle, determined to take everything into its possession. For a long time, Özgür sought an author who exchanged the real but irrational world in which she lived for the fictional, but more real, one.

Finally, she understood that she was the only person capable of giving meaning to the void that surrounded her. Nobody else could decipher life's puzzles for her, or open its padlocks. She started writing on the day that she decided where to deploy her forces against the city's blind violence. Neither for herself nor for others; she wrote simply because she had to. As if excavating a wound, she peeled away the scab, layer by layer, to reveal the reality of Rio, the dark blood spewed by an internally bleeding patient dripping onto each of her sentences.

By the end of her fourth month in Rio, which also marked her encounter with her fourth murder victim, she was already well aware of her mortality; she had accepted that it would take a single bullet to the head, in any street, to wipe her off this earth for good. She'd gotten in line for her own tiny role in a tragedy ongoing since time immemorial, and the words had been given to her only on loan.

"You must go to distant lands to understand people," a writer had once said. Yet Özgür was able to understand the Latins only after she had left them far behind. "*Não vaia; a realidade está dentro de você.*" (Don't go away; reality lies within you). Perhaps she would have to transcend hell before she could be reborn. The perilous, hellish, melancholy tropics...

She'd now spurned that which had been presented to her as "the world;" mobilizing all of her forces, she concentrated upon a single goal—to capture Rio like a butterfly in her hand, and to gently imprison it in her words, without killing it. And so *The City in Crimson Cloak* was born.

A TRAVELER
IN
THE STREETS OF RIO III

The city trembles feverishly in a raging fire. Like a huge beached whale it struggles to breathe, buried beneath the clouds of steam rising from the hot asphalt. Not a single breeze has blown in from the beach for days now; the heat rises as it drifts inland, hitting forty-five in center city. Street dogs foam at the mouth; the street children's lips are cracked from dehydration; the ocean's feeble waves lick at the city's wounds. Only a downpour of light washes the dusty avenues that reek of humans. The raw, sharp, painfully dazzling tropical sunshine protracts colors in a trail of haze. Barely bearable afternoons... Time flying blindly by... The hours squirm, wail, writhe. All bodies are exhausted, sticky, sated to the very last cell. In a slumber that beckons her to death, she tries to gather strength for the night. The day has been abandoned to rot, like a piece of fruit that's had its savory sections consumed.

A Turkish woman wandering aimlessly about the streets of Rio, having taken refuge in her own self, like a snail retreats into its shell; fearing the imminent pistol at her temple; her mouth like sandpaper; taking tremulous steps; large rings of sweat at her armpits... There is nothing she can trust except for her own eyes; the horizon is limited to her gaze. She struggles to drag her pale existence towards the future, which has been repealed here on these savage lands.

She is constantly hungry, but disgusted by food. She is constantly tired, but afraid of nightmares. She is constantly thirsty, but knows not what for. She smokes one cigarette after the other and cannot stop her lips from trembling.

She wants to slip her arm into that of a random passer-by and beg for a word. Not for love, or romance, or friendship; just one word. That single word that will give meaning to all sounds. The weary shadow of her back, entirely incapable of cruelty, brushes past the street people.

DOWNHILL

Reality is an illusion
That we have forgotten is an illusion.
—Derrida

She was making her way down the perilous slope of Santa Teresa and into the city. The road, the sidewalks of which probably hadn't been repaired for some forty years, meandered like the Amazon River, frequently changing direction with its sharp bends. The tramway rails, having absorbed the heat of the summer day, shone like newly sharpened yellow knives and exuded a nauseating metallic scent. Özgür was walking along the railway, which had been out of use since the Japanese businessman was killed. With their worn-out heels, her shoes wouldn't have been able to handle the rough stones of Santa Teresa. She took short, swift steps, like a Japanese woman in a kimono, from one railway tie to the next; now and then she'd jump, as if playing a game of hopscotch. Perhaps the last flicker of childhood that Rio hadn't yet managed to strip her of... She definitely never ever stepped on metal; it was one of numerous personal mini rites she'd developed to protect herself from bad luck. Until just a year ago, she'd turned her nose up at the Brazilians' vacuous beliefs, the countless religions upon which they'd wreaked havoc, all kinds of mystic beliefs to which they half-wittingly devoted themselves—astrology, fortunes, icons, hymns, spells. In this city, so chaotic that a single god alone could never endure, various religions, denominations, and myths mingled and meshed. The Catholic Church, condemning with one hand while sanctifying with the other; Protestantism, a faded patch in the revelry of the tropics; the Baptist Church, with its ceremonies of noise, commotion, and samba spilling over into the

streets; the *Candomblé*, now nothing but black magic; native to-
tems turned into flea market gods; Zen Buddhism, the favorite of
the ecologically concerned new generation middle class, so open
as it is to all kinds of quests for balance; Mormons who climb
up to the *favela*s in dress suits, despite the infernal heat; Hare
Krishnas with their carnival masks... In this life-squandering city,
survival proved impossible for the godless.

The steep incline made construction impossible, and so the
slope on the right side of the hill was a completely unsettled jungle. Only a Franciscan monestary, dating from the end of the last
century, stood concealed behind high walls. Nobody was allowed
to go in, and the nuns were not allowed to leave. Özgür's curious
eyes were only able to pick out a silhouette or two, swaying like
penguins behind the iron door. On the left side were rows of decrepit houses, large and small. Villas, left behind by the pre-coup
rich who had made their escape when the *favela*s took over Santa
Teresa, had rotted and disintegrated in this atrocious climate well
before their time. Weeds, ivy, thorny bushes, fallen tree trunks
had overtaken the derelict yards, and the jungle, reborn each day,
enveloped everything. It looked war-torn; everything strewn,
chaotic, wounded... Visible here and there amongst the savage
greenness gushing forth from every pore, swiftly devouring every
inch into which it could sink its claws, was the craterous Santa
Teresa valley.

The *favelinha* was like a thousand-armed, chalky white octopus
trying to climb its way up a gigantic, deep green crock. Resisting
gravity on those huge rock outcrops, on the soaring cliffs of Rio
where even grass feared to tread, the *favela*s grew, day by day, like
a boil. A monument to desperation, unclear whether it was growth
or decay; an organism with nine lives, a giant accumulation of an-
nexes, comprised of so much hopelessness, so many lost battles,
so much personal agony... Nearly all of the featureless, indistinct

matchbox houses, which looked more like dressing cabins on the beach than places of residence, had been constructed directly adjacent to one another. They had no roofs, and their interlinking terraces provided for a labyrinthine structure that made police raids next to impossible. Except for midday, when they were subjected to the sun's rage, the terraces would teem with people like so many anthills.

Men, carjacking family breadwinners by trade, would prepare pork chops and lug cases of beer for a cookout. Full-bodied mulatto women would hang laundry; adolescents, having partaken of all manner of sexuality and violence before the age of fifteen, would revamp their speakers for the night *festa*. Ghetto children, the only species on earth absolutely impervious to the sun, would swarm about like so many bees escaped from the hive. An image of a peaceful, sedate, domestic Sunday, enough to easily fool anyone not well acquainted with Rio... Yet the shots continued to ring out on the hour, revealing all of this—the chops, the hammocks, the baby clothes drying on the line—to be ephemeral, in the balance, lost. It was but a mask, vital and breathing; and hiding the seeds and memory of death.

A VOYAGER IN THE LAND OF THE DEAD

The favelados *don't call the place where they live the* favela, *just like the Natives don't call themselves Natives. They refer to themselves by a more direct, straightforward term—*morro *(hill). In Portuguese,* morro *also means "I'm dying." So is it just a slip of the tongue, or yet another example of the city's devilish sense of humor?*

The reluctant guide on this journey into the Land of the Dead was a black beauty; a strict Catholic, member of the communist party, university student, hailing from the Vigario Geral *(a* favela *famous for the horrendous massacre that took place there in 1994).* Maria

Theresa ferried them across the Underground River—the gringa, burning with curiosity, and four Cariocas who agreed to go on this journey just because they could not bring themselves to let the gringa go alone, otherwise they would never in this lifetime ever have set foot in a favela.

The Land of the Dead's insidious, squalid, mysterious labyrinths... An hour-long climb that leaves you breathless as you leap from terrace to terrace and rock to rock, passing through the narrowest of corridors and tunnels... Homes, their plaster peeling, looking like faces riddled with pimples and boils; huts drooping to one side, as if melted by the sun; brush and reed shanties from who knows what period of civiliza-tion... Everything functional, jam-packed, huddled, and as ugly as can be. Like theater décor on the verge of collapse; she smelled mud and sewage, and the stench of rotting. She perceived an unnamable being in the throes of death there in the shadows. It was, perhaps, the trag-edies that had been passed down from generation to generation. Dark powers, nightmares, crippling fears, blood-sucking battles, dangerous vibrations...

A sentry every fifty meters. Commando Vermelho's rankless soldiers, Hades' pubescent guards... The sharp eyes of a huge bird of prey always at their back... They wear fat gold chains and watches; on their feet are sneakers the size of babies' tombs; their Bob Marley t-shirts conceal their pistols, the keys that open up all the doors that the world has slammed in their faces. They dress like rap stars, they strut like Hollywood gangsters, and they die like flies. Without even realizing that they themselves are the real gangsters, the real people of the ghetto.

They had been invited to the Fifteenth-birthday party of the daughter of a modest, pious working class family. The young girl, al-ready looking like a mother of two, was swathed in her snow white, heart-rending communion clothes. A lacy dress with a billowy skirt and puff sleeves, pointy, high-soled linen shoes, a crown of fake flow-

ers, etc... Women dressed in an amalgam of bright colors, as if they'd
been doused in buckets of paint, were gathered around a cake decorated with kitschy swans and tacky roses, posing for the photographer,
who'd been hired for this night, a night spared no sacrifice. Some
slapped their most naïve, most imbecilic smiles on their face, while
others slipped out of the mask of happiness they've been forced to
wear throughout their lives, and there in front of the camera arrived
at their solemn, heavy-hearted, exhausted selves, their real selves. An
amazingly familiar world, like those town weddings in old Turkish
movies... A guitar instead of the drum and horn, the samba instead of
the çiftetelli... Some two hundred guests sardined on the large living-
room-sized terrace scrambled for the refreshment and pastry trays as
if their lives depended on it. A privilege, however, was bestowed upon
the gringa, who was handed a stool and a can of soda. She felt like
a giant parrot that hadn't yet learned how to speak; perched on her
stool, she took microscopic sips from her soda, which was as warm
as the water at a Turkish bath, and tried to withstand the heat and
the sweaty bodies that pressed up against her. At one point, knowing
well and good that she would lose her goldmine of a spot in the corner,
she asked for leave from two gangsters at the head of the stairs and
dove indoors, only to find that it was even more crowded inside than it
had been out on the terrace. Women of all ages clustered in groups of
ten or fifteen in the mostly windowless rooms the size of monks' cells
gazing at black and white screens under the raw light of naked bulbs.
There was no running water; the electricity was stolen; cardboard and
linoleum were plastered all over the windows and there was a television in every room. Neither the boundaries of the house were clear,
nor its doors, or who came and went. In the favelas reigned a lifestyle
that rendered concepts like "property" and "private life" and taboos
like incest invalid; but more than a commune it resembled a women's
prison ward. When the famished guest of honor took a pastry from
one of the trays in the kitchen, she met with harsh glances, sharp re-

proaches, blatant curses. The insolent bourgeois, claiming every object
on earth, touching and grasping and fingering everything they can get
their hands on!

Before the hour of midnight, the small group was told to leave the
favela immediately. Of course there was no explanation, but the word
on the town was that a bloodbath was underway in Boca de Fuma
(Smoke Mouth), where the cocaine dealing went on.

Final image from the Land of the Dead: The group, abandoned by
their guide midway, is horrified, and desperately seeks a way out; they
throw themselves downhill and run with all their might. They dive into
dead end streets, climb walls, jump from roof to roof. Some trip and
fall on the rough streets, some bawl their eyes out, some remember
their manhood and curse their cowardice... Each one is concerned with
saving himself alone; nobody helps anyone else; nobody encourages
anyone else, nobody turns around to look after the others. A salvo of
semi-automatics rings out from uphill. A breathless Eurydice, drenched
as if she'd been washed down with a hose, is so taken aback that she
forgets to be afraid; with all her might she tries to catch up; she falls
down twice and, desensitized to the pain in her swollen ankle, skips
from stone to stone like a broken-winged sparrow. She is on the verge
of wetting herself.

Down, downhill, down as if she would never stop... Don't stop, not
even for a second, don't lose the herd, gather all your strength! Don't
fall again and, whatever you do, do not look back!

In her novel she had recorded, true to actual events, an account
of the journey that she had made back in the spring of ninety-
four, to the huge *favela* of Vigario Geral, where masked policemen massacred two homes full of people; that is, true except for
one small detail. Actually, she hadn't heard any gunshots that
night; she'd received news of the fight in *Boca de Fuma* only later.
Unfortunately, all those horrifying nightmares do eventually

come true! The headline on the violence page last Sunday: "10 dead in Vigario Geral. Cocaine war crashes birthday party."

Another one of those curves in which her novel, instead of chasing breathlessly after the truth as it usually does, suddenly sprints ahead to take the lead. To her it was perfectly natural that after transferring them to paper, she should recall her memories just as she had written them, or that language should replace a slice of reality that had already taken place. Human memory, let alone a writer's memory, possesses not a shred of that virtue called honesty. But what was really frightening was the prescience of her imaginings. And how they claimed some sort of right over the future... The real Rio de Janeiro and The City in Crimson Cloak had melded together, both in time and space; they had become a unified, insoluble, unparsable whole, as much in the future as in the past. And the labyrinth, with all of its wells and pendulums and secret rooms, through which she fumbled and groped her way, was as much internal as it was external.

At one point she had endeavored to write a book that was one hundred percent autobiographical. Or as she once referred to it on a particularly sarcastic day, "a record of traumatic events." Perhaps it was her attempt to knock a tragic hero, a proud monument of humankind, off its pedestal... Her goal: to polish up those memories, frozen in the placenta of her imagination, with a coat of poeticism. Yet what had emerged was a completely different story altogether; a story that, even if it had "happened to her," was not something that she had "experienced" for real, but a story that belonged to another woman, to Ö. That intractable woman whose progress she so carefully monitored, like a mother listening to her baby kick in her womb, was growing increasingly independent with every passing day, and kept trying to take over the author's own role; she was usurping center stage. It was as if Özgür's bland soul had been held up to a prism, and in the form

of Ö., finally radiated with all the colors of the spectrum, even in
the purest, most pristine black and white. As if she were more
concrete, more real, more human than Özgür. More alive, even
after being murdered by a single bullet near the Blue Hill *favela* at
the end of the novel. Finally, in the end, once she'd grown strong
enough, she would break free, pushing Özgür onto the margins
and overtaking her completely. She would set out for the savage
lands of her own country—dragging her maker behind her, like a
shadow...

She walked silently up the hill for some time, breaking out in a
tar-like sweat beneath the sharp lights, which bit at the back of her
neck. She'd swiftly used up the little bit of energy that the *guaraná*
had provided. Her head began to spin and she became nauseated
before she'd even made it halfway up the hill. The asphalt was
melting beneath her feet. Two years ago, in Copacabana, she had
tried to swim in the ocean for the very first—and very last—time.
Immersed in freezing water up to her waist, she waited for that
first wave to hit her. For that huge ocean wave, maybe a meter
high, which quickly rose before her like a wall of steel, wreaking
havoc as it drew closer... She'd stood firm as a rock, and did not
collapse. Not for a long time, not until the wave began to recede,
taking the floor below her feet with it. She was hit by another
wave, a ferocious kick to the face, and then another, before she'd
had the chance to recompose herself... And that's exactly how she
felt right now; the world was receding below her feet. And she
knew why: HUNGER. She hadn't had anything to eat for the last
twenty-four hours.

She quickly scouted out her surroundings before slipping into
the garden of the long disused villa belonging to the Society for
the Protection of Street Children. She took a few steps into the
thick brush and then withdrew to a secluded area invisible from
the road. She took out her pocket mirror, her five *real* banknote,

and the cocaine in her stash. She wiped her damp palms on her pants; with skillful fingers she made two fine lines of powder on the mirror; she leaned towards her own reflection, like an elephant leaning in to drink water from a lake, a paper trunk hanging from her nose. It sent a dose of pure, undiluted, false energy into her body, which was depleted of strength or desire to walk any further. The cocaine seared her nasal passages as if she'd just inhaled nitric acid; she squeezed her nose with all of her might to make sure that not one bit of her featherweight friend went to waste.

She didn't have enough money to be a coke addict, and besides, she didn't really enjoy it anyway. In Rio, shed of all of their associated myths, drugs had become an object of consumption equally accessible to one and all. They were easier to get than bread even. Everyone in Carioca did them; from servants to businessmen, from university professors to police chiefs. Drugs kept the *favelas* afloat, invigorated the city's economy, and paid for the unfathomable costs of the carnival. For a long time she had avoided cocaine like the plague. She was prone to all kinds of addictions, especially when alone and idle. Over time her willpower weakened, and her indifference towards herself increased to such a degree that nothing frightened her anymore. She experienced the miraculous transformation she'd been hoping for only once, only the first time she'd tried it. Suddenly, she had become as light as a feather; she'd shed her chronic unhappiness, and the heavy armor of her dour personality. At the hour of midnight she'd thrown herself into the task of housecleaning, which she'd been putting off for months, and was finished in half an hour. Still feeling the rush, she'd then proceeded to look through all of the old newspapers, letters, and scraps of paper lying about, to organize her bookshelf, to kill the leeches in her bathtub, and finally to dress herself up to the nines before dashing out of her apartment. Until the wee hours of morning she'd hopped from

bar to bar, belting out songs and dancing to the world's most challenging rhythms, from the *samba* to the *axé*, and getting frisky
with a blue-eyed mulatto while waiting in the never-waning line
for the bathroom at Sobrenatural.

Now she used that winged elixir from the Andes solely for
the purpose of coping with the grueling effects of hunger. For
some time she hadn't been on very good terms with drugs or
alcohol anyway. And she was not concerned with escaping from
the real world—if such a thing does indeed exist. To the contrary, she hopelessly tried to draw closer to it. Before her stood a
Matryoshka, countless dolls nested one inside the other; but try
as she might, she just could not reach that world at the bottom,
the essence, the core of reality.

The battle at the top of Santa Teresa had started up once again.
The gangsters must have woken from their siestas and gotten
back to work, mumbling and cursing and groggy. A round of bullets, silence, another round. Bullets that turn the serene face of
the afternoon into one seared with pockmarks... "Like me, these
fellas probably just have no patience for the familial atmosphere
of Sundays," thought Özgür, smiling beneath a synthetic halo of
happiness. "There you have it, the real world! In all its magnificence, unfolding like a fan before my very eyes... Semi-automatics, senseless conversation, lunatics... A torchlight procession of
jesters!" All of a sudden she doubled over, as if she'd just been
given a swift kick to the stomach. That awful nausea, the most
tenacious gift this generous city had given her...

She'd managed to make it through another Rio carnival
without being violated, trampled, mugged, stabbed, or raped.
For ten days and nights, overcome with a case of stark raving
madness, the locals, together with a few thousand tourists
flabbergasted by the downpour of tits and ass, had staged the
world's most grandiose orgy. Özgür, too, had gotten caught

up in the overpowering current of events. In the forty-degree heat, *blocos* (throngs of masked and unmasked people raising hell, making love, drinking, dancing, and trailing after musicians perched on the backs of trucks) had besieged the city like throngs of marauders, and she had run from one *bloco* to the next. She made room for one body amongst the thousands of wet bodies pouncing upon her; she'd taken her life into her own hands just to wriggle to the samba and twisted her ankle while bouncing about to the *frevo*; she hadn't protested at the pinches to her ass, and had only sought help from the police two or three times when things really got out of hand. She, too, snatched a few of the one million condoms being passed out in front of the Sambódromo— souvenirs of Rio—and watched scenes that surpassed anything her well-behaved imagination could ever have conjured up, as if peeping on a bunch of mating cats... She'd been pulled into that dizzying, magnetic field of sexuality; for ten days and ten nights she'd been hurled from one extreme to the next in a state of semi-insanity. She was breathless, drenched, and stunned, like a baby bird that's fallen into a swamp... The frozen corpse smile that she stuck on her face in lieu of a carnival mask; a can of cola and a packet of cigarettes always in hand; her keys attached to her underwear with safety pins; lacking identity, willpower, ego... And when, finally, she could no longer stand the loneliness of carnival, a loneliness like no other, she threw herself into the nearest lap. Indiscriminately... Throughout all those days and nights she had spent scared to death of being attacked, catching a disease, or losing her mind, she had failed to convince herself, even once, that she was happy; or more precisely, that this was happiness. With one exception, just a single brief moment... That indescribable, inexpressible, unrepeatable moment, there in that pile of recollections that memory should have immediately relegated to the trash bin...

On the last night, she had given in. Unable to find a quiet place to weep in that huge, sprawling city, she'd run home, where she suffered nervous attacks for hours on end, and puked and puked until morning.

CARNIVAL

Rio had become a mask without a face, a huge subconscious covered in gold dust. The city trembled, shook, collapsed all around, as if an enormous mine were caving in beneath it. Bodies all moving to the same, single rhythm; with their rough kisses, the sudden surging and ebbing of dancers, the beat of the atabaque *drums, the synchronic swaying of bodies intertwined like ivy.*

It's like climbing towards the summit of a mountain range; just when you think you've reached it, with its long, elegant, merciless finger, Rio points to another pinnacle of madness.

The real world and the dream world had been reversed. Women in men's clothes, men in women's clothes; transvestites in netted stockings, g-strings, and stiletto heels wearing Reagan and Thatcher masks; sequined dresses shimmering in the dark night, parrot feathers, confetti, fireworks; fake penises, inflated breasts, shiny fetishes; police passing out cocaine on the corner and gangsters out on patrol; housewives emulating prostitutes, and prostitutes emulating nuns; phosphorescent bodies dyed in a spectrum of bright colors, dipped in gilding, whitewashed; Nazi army officers, Julius Caesars, pharaohs, titans, Apollo and Dionysus, bull masks, bear masks, African gods, Amazonian deities, clowns, jesters, acrobats, and most of all Carmens, Aphrodites, Cleopatras, catwomen, panther women, and tiger women... Adolf Hitler and a mulatto transvestite in tights dancing the overture to an amorous wrestling match. Tutankhamen getting it on with Marilyn Monroe. A short-winded, wobbly-legged John Wayne running after the candy apples. Desire, driven to extremes only to be-

come a parody of itself... Costumes that seem hollow, bodies that look like wall decoration, masks without faces behind them... But still there was a moment, even in this fairground of lust... A moment in which all of the masks began breathing, and fingers touching the canvas could feel the naked human skin...

The parade in Sambódromo is about to begin. Breath is bated as everyone waits for the bateria. *The five hundred drummers of the first samba school are gathering strength for the over one hour long parade; bags of cocaine by the pound are passed around from person to person. They're all black, all from the favela; they are neither freer nor wealthier than their grandfathers who were brought over to the New World in slave ships. Now it is only in the beat of their pulse that they are able to capture the vast savannah that exists somewhere over there beyond the horizon, their war dances, the dark, naked gods that they betray with the crosses around their necks... And the music begins...*

A thousand arms, a thousand arms hardened by the ruthless sun and the even more ruthless whip, begin beating the drums all at once. The sound of the bateria *can be heard from miles away; it draws closer, and closer, and finally swells to infinite proportions and clasps the night in its fist. It climbs up knees and hips; takes hold of hands; wraps around lips; and explodes at the very core of one's ego. Hundreds of thousands of people packed into the Sambódromo jump to their feet and interlock. Some scream, some yell at the top of their lungs, some grow ecstatic, some kick and stamp their feet... Like a wave rising from the depths of the ocean, a powerful force is exuded by the hundreds of thousands now transformed into pure flesh, the center of gravity of one body. The impulsive force of life, older than history, older than the word... The slave is conquering the master. And the dance begins. "Screaming, drums, dance, dance, dance, dance!"*

If there is a pinnacle of madness, this must be it. Existence, waning as it rises, to disintegrate in the bosom of nothingness. A kind of obliteration subsuming even death... And that, alas, is the ultimate descent; the one that destroys itself along with everything else.

In the secluded garden that she referred to as her "tropical nook," she leaned her head against her knees and fought the nausea, biting her hands until they nearly bled. It was as if bullets were ripping through her head. The cocaine hadn't done her taut nerves—so taut they were about to snap—any good. "I need a little peace of mind, some peace of mind, and to forget. The sound of gunshots separates me even from my very self now; those and that cursed novel." She was in the jungle, that corner of the world farthest from any kind of peace of mind. Hundreds of insects, flies, and ants had descended upon her; they seemed to be waiting for the damp, odd-smelling, motionless mass of meat to disintegrate any moment now. She was surrounded by plants intertwined, shoulder to shoulder, crammed together. Racing towards the sun, always higher and higher, with a rabid thirst for light; in a state of constant bickering, always at each other's throats, seeming to explode from within as they gave vent to their frustration... Each leaf was the incarnation of another battle, like every bullet and every word... The sign of another death, yet another mask...

Some slightly wilted orchids caught her eye. Six orchids were lined up in a crescent moon shape around a half-smoked cigar. *MACUMBA*! Black magic! Those forests of Rio still permeable by humans were full of votives offered to the *Candomblé* gods: a half-drunk bottle of *cachaça* or a half-smoked cigar surrounded by six or twelve flowers. Sometimes a pan half-filled with meat or fish. She didn't know the meaning behind the incomplete state of the votive offerings; perhaps the idea was to show that the world belonged to both the gods and the mortals, as if sliced perfectly in half. She remembered that Commando Vermelho came down from the *favelas* at night to bury the dead in abandoned yards and the thought suddenly made her feel uneasy, though neither the corpses nor the black magic could do her any harm. Like the savage tribes, she took no offense at sharing the land with the dead; in fact, she felt herself to be just as privy to the secrets of the dead as the magicians themselves were. Nevertheless, she leapt to her feet. More out of anxiety that she might get scared than out of fear itself, she quickly gathered her bag and began running straight towards the wall. She stood directly in front of it before taking an ostentatious leap and breaking out in uproarious laughter at her groundless fears. A joy filched from childhood! When she was eight or nine years old—twenty long years ago!—she and her neighborhood friends used to hold "pirate expeditions" to the old wooden villas in Göztepe; they'd return from the ruined buildings, long fallen subject to the sultanate of rats, with their booty. Once, they got caught by a watchman. Screaming, hands and arms covered in scratches and bruises, half drunk on the thrill of finally getting to be real pirates, they broke the windows on the second floor and jumped down into the gardens below. Only one person got caught that day. Tiny Özgür, with blood trickling down her knees and onto her ankles, was collared while scrambling to climb over the garden wall. She got a royal thrashing, but she didn't feel any pain. Not only did her punishment intensify the pleasure of having committed a crime, but it elevated her to the rank of martyr.

She stopped at the top of the stairs leading down to Lapa and looked at the Santa Teresa Valley one last time, like Robinson Crusoe bidding farewell to his island. She took a mental photograph of the tropics, one that she could take with her and enlarge any time she wished. Trees whose trunks had become invisible, concealed by clusters of leaves; petulant grasses, lush and dense and full of sap; ivy crawling over everything it could sink its claws into; plump, pint-sized banana trees; imposing mango trees, their tops stroking the sky; bulky jackfruit, the plane tree of the trop-

ics; garrulous palms, their lips in constant mumbling motion...
The rare foreign tree that thinks it's in the Alps, its lanky skeleton visible behind diseased leaves... Like a ballerina holding her
breath, struggling to keep her balance during an extraordinarily
difficult pose. Every tone of green: emerald, pine, pistachio, sea,
apple, jade, chrysolite... The landscape before her was completely
different from the insular, reserved, downcast nature of the
northern climates. Here, nature was so exuberant, so vigorous
and beckoning, so vibrant, that it seemed to be visibly breathing. It wasn't posing for some manmade portrait. It had not yet
been depleted or made into a sacred playground of the goddess.
It had never been part of any established system. It was independent and strong-willed; in a state of constant revolt, refusing to
compromise, pressing forward like a forest fire certain to go out
should it deplete its essence.

"If only I could take in all of these impressions before turning
them into symbols. If only I could keep from imputing my own
emotions to nature, which actually has none." At that moment
she was startled by the eerie sound of someone whistling, as if
a huge tropical bird had just spread its wings right behind her.
Reluctantly, she turned around. There wasn't a soul to be seen
on the hill, which dissolved into a liquid blur before her eyes. She
stood beneath a jackfruit tree; such a sound couldn't possibly
have come from the steel-skinned, rugby-ball-sized fruits at her
feet. She'd tasted jackfruit once. At her tongue's first contact, she
thought it tasted like damson; but then when she ripped into it
with her teeth, it released a bitter, pungent, urine scented juice.
This fruit was the perfect candidate to be a symbol for so many
things; love, life, reality...

"Hey, hey. Over here!"

Her heart leapt into her mouth. Until then, she hadn't noticed the five- or six-year-old black girl sitting on the wall on the

other side of the scrub. She was very cute, tiny and as black as a Senegalese. Her hair was woven, the feisty, fidgety curls tamed into hundreds of skinny African braids. She was wearing make-up; the brick-colored lipstick that she had so generously applied on and around her lips made her mouth look like an open wound.

"Look! Look here! I'm a goalie."

She merrily waved her hands clad in black leather gloves nearly half as big as she was. For a few moments, Özgür was speechless.

"Those aren't goalie gloves. They're boxing gloves," she said finally.

The little girl scowled and stuck out her lower lip. She wasn't one to give up easily.

"These are Pele's gloves."

"That's right. But isn't Pele a boxer?"

The girl gave Özgür a curious look, scanning her from head to toe. There was something weird about this woman, about the way she talked, the way she looked... Some difference that she just couldn't quite put her finger on...

"You're really white," she said after a while, obviously exhilarated at having found an explanation.

For a fleeting moment Özgür considered teaching the girl the word "*gringa*," but quickly changed her mind. Instead, she just smiled.

"Do you like black?" the girl asked.

"What's 'black'?"

Of course she knew very well that the word *preto* meant both black as in the color black, and negro. Ever since she'd started making a living off of private lessons, she'd acted upon this irrepressible urge to ask wretchedly simple questions, behavior which inevitably made her conversants skeptical about her mental health. It wasn't that she was being bratty, but that she was obsessed with analyzing concepts down to their most basic meanings. But lo and behold, the girl wasn't dumbstruck by this question as her students would have been; she countered instantly.

"Black's my color."

Özgür nodded her head in agreement.

"Yes, I like black. And you, do you like my color? White?"

The girl preferred silence to a lie. For several minutes she stared at her gloves, as if wishing to crawl inside them and fall asleep. Then all of a sudden she jumped off the wall and disappeared into the brush.

"Hey, little one! You forgot your gloves! Hey, where'd you go? I've got your gloves here!"

Turning a deaf ear to the instinctual voice that told her to turn around and walk away, Özgür walked up to the wall. Just as she'd thought, the girl had vanished, as if the earth had just swallowed her up. This was really very strange, very strange indeed! Maybe a bad omen. She threw the gloves to the ground like a couple of dead rats. She'd begun to feel dizzy and sick to her stomach again, and her lips were trembling.

"God, please just let me make it through this day in one piece!"

She slowly began to make her descent down the stairs. She could hardly keep her balance, as if she were trying to remain standing on a raft being whisked away by a spontaneous current. Only a few minutes had passed before she paused, closed her eyes, and repeated her ejaculatory prayer three times. Then, before she even had a chance to step aside, she found herself squatting down right there in the middle of the stairs, where she vomited up everything, every last drop and morsel that had entered her stomach that day.

A TRAVELER IN THE STREETS OF RIO
— THE STREET PEOPLE OF RIO

Scenes from the streets of Rio: An eighteen-year-old black girl, black polish on her finger- and toenails, living with her three children, cardboard box, and sponge bed at the entrance of a supermarket in Botafogo. A nine-year-old girl washing the hair of her baby doll in the park in Cinelándia... She hasn't spoken with anyone since she was rescued from the clutches of the prostitution mafia; her eyes are murky, as if someone's pulled velvet drapes over them... An odd bird found only in Rio is perched upon the branches of a mango tree in Flamengo: Who knows who placed this freak, missing the lower half of his body, up there; he talks with his hands, and plays chess with invisible pieces. The man with gangrene waving his tin can as he begs for money in Lapa... He sings songs, recites prayers and hymns, swinging his shoulders in a dance all his own, long ago driven mad by the pain. Passers-by hold their noses to avoid the rank stench of his leg.

Street people are the natural vegetation of the streets of Rio, which are either covered in dust or knee-high pools of mud, depending upon the season. They're strewn everywhere from the palm-lined avenues of touristy Copacabana to the out-of-the-way, wretched slums, taking up residence in the squares, overpasses, and church, hotel, restaurant, and apartment building entrances, like so many marbles that some traveler walking through the streets of Rio had pulled out of her huge bag and randomly scattered about. Thousands, hundreds of thousands of roulette balls hurled beyond the sphere of humanity with the centrifugal force of the wheel of civilization... Thousands, hundreds of thousands of people...

*Handless and armless, elephant-legged, wooden-legged ghouls,
their heads wrapped in bandages, looking as if they've just gotten out
of Auschwitz; brutal, stunted adolescents running around in gangs;
half-grown girls who get raped on every God given day of their lives;
broken-winged pregnant women coping with hunger for two all by
themselves; half-wits wrapped in rags who like skunks mark their ter-
ritories with the odorous clouds that extend around them for yards;
child beggars covered in war wounds, fire wounds, and torture wounds;
elementary-school-aged children with tuberculosis, trachoma, AIDS...
Raving lunatics who talk to themselves, burst out in laughter, mas-
turbate, hurl profanities—deserved, definitely well-deserved—at
the humanity represented by passers-by... The elderly, clinging on to
this world with their rotten teeth, while everyone else eagerly waits
for them to bite the dust as soon as possible... The lords of homeless
societies divided into castes: Claim jumpers, thieves, pickpockets,
mafia errand boys, informers... The "honorably working" middle class:
selling tickets, tokens, coconut candy, guarána soda, and batida from
behind hand-me-down display counters... Families bound by the bonds
of incest, intricately intertwining like ivy, neither the number, nor the
ages, not the parentage of their children known for certain... Beggars
struggling to wrangle every day, hour, minute they can out of Rio's
nearly zero degree mercy...*

*And then there are those who are so done for, they're not even fit
to beg anymore. On the verge of starvation, they have arrived at the
purest, simplest state of existence: mere living matter... They sleep
constantly, day and night, spread out on the sidewalk, or reclining in
pools of mud, on wet concrete, or on the sizzling asphalt. They sleep
constantly, utterly impervious to the onslaught of tropical rains that
continues unabated for weeks, the lethal sun, buses, the police, and
the people who step over them, bump their legs, and sometimes curse,
and sometimes leave a slice of moldy bread. It's a sleep that gradually
grows deeper, heavier, clotted; a slow, fitful journey to the border of*

the Land of the Dead... *Their deaths are always silent, like a candle extinguished by the wind. A death unencumbered by prayers, hymns, or bugles. They don't yell, they don't scream, they don't rebel. Because there is nobody who will listen to them. They only resist. With that oldest, most desperate, most indomitable passion of the body, a will as tough as steel, laying claim to that sliver of life still left within them, they resist, and resist, and resist...*

NOTE: *The settled people of Rio are so disgusted by these reptiles that ruin their views, turn their beautiful city into a veritable open-air toilet, a hospital, a concentration camp, that thoroughly ruin their reputation in the eyes of foreigners and keep them from wandering the streets without fear, that they lavish the* justiceiros *with money. It doesn't cost more than three, five hundred dollars to do away with a purse-snatching street kid loitering at a kiosk. But in the pre-carnival season, when it's a matter of tourist safety and national pride, prices may rocket up to as much as double the standard rates.*

THE
NEW WORLD

Death is the only thing
That remains unwritten.
—Robert Pinget

Ever since the military coup, the back streets of Lapa, Rio's oldest neighborhood, had been in the hands of the homeless, transvestites, and footloose ex-cons. Once the shops selling auto equipment, electronics, spare parts, knives, and guns pulled down their metal shutters and secured their huge padlocks, the charming mulatto belles in their g-strings and net stockings, and the murderous-looking men who lived off them, would take over. Even a worldly-wise migrant like Özgür would have a hard time pounding the pavement of these streets, which served men twenty-four hours a day. The most savage metropolis of Europe was like a Boy Scout camp compared to Rio. But the only stop where she could catch the Santa Teresa bus was located here, on a street lined from one end to the other with kiosk-bar mutts known as "luncheonettes." In Rio, which lacked a café culture and had a climate unsuitable for indoor spaces, on every corner you could find a luncheonette, each one like a gaping dent chipped into the wall, or a fake cave carved into a building, lacking a door or four walls to define it. They were the center of gravity in the gastronomic life of the city. Customers would lean on the long counters while they ate and drank, or settle into the fold-up tables and chairs that covered the sidewalks on those sizzling hot summer nights. Though once they had been equidistant, over time Özgür's soul had become even less adapted to the tropics than her body had. It was only now that she understood the vital importance of being able to sit in a tea garden or a café for hours on end. Or of having

breakfast standing up... It made her throw in the towel immediately in her duello with each new day, inevitably armed as it was
with a fresh gamut of traps, nastiness, fracas, lies, and deceit.

Dozens of street people lived below the one-hundred-fifty-
year-old stone bridge, which was just wide enough for a single
tram to pass. A little farther along, next to Lapa Square, was a
grandiose conservatory, its wall covered from top to bottom in a
colorful Rio gravure. Golden beaches; sharp cliffs thumbing their
noses at the sky; statues of Jesus, those permanent fixtures of Rio
postcards, suspended in the air by some invisible force and looking as if they might fall flat on their faces any minute; a gigantic
spear of fire flung fiercely out of the heavens, dividing the city
straight down the middle; and the seven arrows of the rainbow
embedded in the ocean... Meanwhile, on the other side stood a
series of rundown buildings left over from Lapa's glory days. A
few of them were repaired with state money and donated to ART,
which hardly has a say in these parts. A concert hall, an Afro-
Brazilian cultural center, the street theater called *Ta Na Rua*... The
Olenewa studio, founded by a Russian ballerina who, like Özgür,
arrived in the New World with a single suitcase and pale white
northern skin...

Just as it is possible to find a nook of one's own even in hell
itself, in this city Özgür took refuge in the wooden, two-story
ballet school. A safe harbor where she could cast anchor during
days otherwise spent adrift in nothingness... In Rio she eagerly
embraced this ever so aristocratic, ever so European art form that
she'd abandoned years ago; turning it into a vital ceremony, which,
though it may have lost its essence, still preserved its form. Its
corridors filled with the scent of resin, the sound of piano tunes,
and perfectly postured, wafer-thin girls scurrying about like
frightened pigeons, the Olenewa Studio was like any other ballet
school in the world; initially, however, Özgür had been dazzled

by those particular details of the Studio unique to the tropics. For example, the road from the dressing room to the classrooms passed through a garden of mango trees and when the rainy season began, it would be covered in water puddles from one end to the next. Buckets were placed in the classrooms to gather the rain streaming in from the roof, and the drops that snuck in through the windows, which wouldn't quite close all the way, would slap the dancers' sweaty shoulders. With the onset of the hot months, the arbor in the garden would fill up with monkeys jumping from branch to branch, and beautiful dark-skinned girls waiting in line for ice cream. And then there was the half-cracked, sickly cat, a male tabby which, despite having grown up amongst humans, never became domesticated; it would wander the corridors grumbling about this and that, lashing out in reproach at every Tom, Dick, and Harry it happened to run into, as if to say, "With life as awful as it is right now, and all you people do is waste your energy trying to stand on your toes!"

Three nights a week she'd walk out of her ballet lesson, and— with the sound of Chopin's waltzes flitting in her ears, exhausted, her tongue stuck to the roof of her dry mouth, but having undergone enough spiritual cleansing to endure the streets of Rio for a while longer—she'd slowly make her way to Ernesto. She'd let her imagination get carried away as she envisioned that first fruit juice; the occasion assumed the allure of a sexual fantasy, and she would derive a delicate pleasure from putting off her papaya-orange cocktail, that elixir of life, as long as possible. The sounds of *pagôda* and *samba* rhythms would begin to emerge from the back streets at those hours, and the impatient couples at the Afro-Brazilian Center would leap to their feet for the opening dance.

Ernesto was the only Copacabana-style restaurant in Lapa, which means it was a run-of-the-mill restaurant with a door, four walls, and air conditioning that hit you like a cold shower as soon as you walked in. (She'd spent her first few months in Rio in a state of constant illness because of those air conditioners. In the month of May, dressed in spring apparel, the instant plunge from forty degrees to fifteen was like suddenly getting caught up in a snowstorm. Who would've believed that she'd have to carry a sweater with her at all times in the hottest city in the world?) Locals never eat dinner alone in Rio, and so Ernesto, like all the other pretentious restaurants in the city, did not offer single servings. Özgür would grow red in the face as she asked to have half of her meal doggy-bagged for the next night's dinner, and nearly apologize for her incurable loneliness. Friday nights were especially crowded at Ernesto. Students from the conservatory, musicians, people off to the theater, cinema, or opera... Laughter rolling out in bursts like oceanic waves, increasing in proportion with the amount of beer consumed... A blind piano player wearing sunglasses, much effort having been invested in his Ray Charles look, played such trite tunes as "Autumn Leaves" and "Strangers in the Night," to which no one paid any attention, except for Özgür and a few old drunks. No matter how resigned she was not to give in to cheap sentimentalism, Özgür couldn't stop the tears from welling up in her eyes. Her loneliness would spread throughout her body like a pain with no known source, and her need to love and be loved would become a matter of life or death. She'd convince herself that love was the only thing that made life compassionate, meaningful, or at least bearable. And sometimes, if she was having a lucky day, a familiar face passing by would notice Özgür's somber profile on the other side of the glass and come in to chat with her for the duration of a beer. No matter who it was, the son of her former landlord, the cashier from the super-market, a nameless face she'd met months before at a concert, he would wrap her up in a warm embrace and grow livelier and more talkative by the minute. Lonely people always talk too much. Yet such miracles (fleeting and unimportant, but miracles nonetheless!) would disappear just as quickly as they had appeared; the "buddy" in question would grow tired of the *gringa*'s impossible Portuguese enunciation, her vexingly slow speech, and her lack of knowledge—she knew nothing of Veloso's latest record or what time the Ipanema concert was—and would soon head off on his way, but only after having invited her to an outdoor party or a dance hall, as decorum would have it... Özgür would feel lonelier, more defeated, more exhausted than ever. She'd review the superficial conversation in her head once again, laugh to herself at a few of the jokes she'd made, and well up with pride at having told an oft-repeated story with a little more finesse this time around. Finally, she would curse Rio for making her beg for such vapid crumbs of communication, and, at the pinnacle of self-destruction, she would escape to the Afro-Brazilian Cultural Center in search of easily obtainable physical consolation.

At that moment, more than anything else she needed Ernesto's calm, peaceful atmosphere, impervious to pain as it was, just like an old musical. A fortress that neither chaos nor the jungle nor the *samba* could penetrate... The cramps in her stomach had not yet subsided; her nasal passages were still on fire from the cocaine. What she wouldn't do for a heavenly-scented papaya juice with a few chunks of ice swimming inside... Two dollars and twenty cents! "Luncheonette's the only place fit for a pauper like me," she thought. "I get thirsty every fifteen minutes anyway." She decided to buy a forty-cent cup of coffee at O *Novo Mundo* (The New World) and delve back into her green notebook. She needed to pick up from where she'd left off and continue writing *Point Zero*.

A mulatto in his twenties was lying on the sidewalk; he'd fallen asleep leaning against one of the columns that stood in for a door at The New World. He had a startlingly handsome face, with an expression like that of a young boy, surprisingly innocent for someone living on the streets. She felt like covering him with a blanket and planting a goodnight kiss on his cheek. She'd made her way up the misshapen step when she realized that the young man's legs were swollen like a couple of dead dolphins. Elephantiasis! During the dry season, the legs of street people would swell up like gourds and be covered in festering wounds. During the final stages of the illness, they would no longer be able to walk and, resigning themselves to a spot in front of a restaurant or luncheonette, they would entrust their lives to the very limited, and unreliable, mercy of humankind. It had been three or four months since she'd encountered that well groomed woman with the beautiful, made-up face. The woman had been sitting in front of the same column, on a skateboard-like piece of wood with wheels; from the waist down, she was no more. On her clean, white t-shirt it said, JESUS LOVES YOU. It was Tolstoy who believed that love and benevolence made the world go round, right? Özgür had started praying again; an uncontrollable urge prompted her to repeat the same words every time she encountered some beaten or wounded person, especially one missing a limb. Three times. A simple refrain calling upon her personal god, from whom she herself no longer really expected much assistance, to help THEM. On some days she saw so many of them that she spent almost the entirety of her long walk praying. A psychologist, a psychologist who had never been to Rio, could easily have explained the situation as a "fear of castration" and, unfortunately, may have been right in his assessment.

She staggered her way inside. Struggling with the dizziness and the nausea, she took big, boisterous, cowboy steps (like she always did when walking into such places). Despite its highfalutin name, The New World, the most popular three-star hotel in Rio was just another hole in the wall, a glorified luncheonette. Four or five wobbly tables were lined up next to the now-gray ceramic tiled wall. She thought the restaurant, long and narrow with its low ceiling, dark at all hours, looked like a submarine. And so she'd nicknamed it "Nautilus." The combination of water seeping out from beneath the doors of the toilet, which was always kept locked, and the increasingly potent stench of burnt grease, rotten oranges, and beer as one progressed inside, did not really make for an appetizing locale. As if to spite Ernesto, which was just two steps down the way, The New World's clientele consisted of bums, "been there, done that's," pimps, and jailbirds. Unlike those well-bred kids doing their best to look lawless, or the middle class milk-and-water rogues, these were real criminals just trying to look normal. They kept their cover, never got caught red-handed, and balanced their perfectly flat, shallow worlds on their guns. The only other regulars at The New World were the police. And the only difference between them and the "criminals" they fought tooth and nail for a slice of the market pie was that their guns were on display for all to see. Otherwise they had the same dark, sepulchral eyes, the same gaze, drunk on power and brimming over with the blood they'd consumed... It was Rio that had shown Özgür that order and chaos were inseparably bound to one another. The criminal world that she had once exalted with that romanticism indoctrinated by movies had now become nothing but a common, repulsive detail of her daily life.

Her gaze steady ahead, Özgür did a quick reconnaissance out of the corners of her eyes, taking in no more, and no less, than necessary. The relative calmness of Sunday evening had permeated this place, too; there wasn't a soul in the joint except for a group of drunkards, all of them black, entertaining themselves at a table in the very back. Armando, the only waiter who didn't look at Özgür with invasive, greasy, derisive eyes, was standing behind the counter, placing fresh-out-of-the-oven *cochibas*—chicken legs rolled in cassava starch and then fried—on a tray. He hadn't ripped Özgür off, not even once, in the whole two years she'd been there; he'd always brought her her change right away, exact down to the penny, and had patiently taught her the menu in those days when her Portuguese was pitifully poor, and even wrote checks for her sometimes. (Back then nobody used cash because of the inflation rate, which hovered at several thousand percent.)

Silent as a shadow she slipped into a seat at a table, its white paper tablecloth covered in huge tomato sauce stains left behind by previous customers. She had her back to the toilet and the group of drunkards. But no matter how hard she tried, she could not make herself invisible! Before she'd even had a chance to catch her breath, she heard a woman's voice, harsh, cracked, the words rolling in her mouth like hot potatoes.

"Hey, looky there, our *GRINGA*'s back! Did you guys know she has a black lover?"

It was the retired whore, now too old to ply her trade, that Özgür used to run into almost every night at Lapa back when she and Roberto were together. She was one of the extras in *The City in Crimson Cloak*. The final link in the chain of coincidences had now fallen into place. She'd placed a fictional conversation between Ö. and this woman in the chapter about the party in Santa Teresa held in honor of Nelson Mandela's election. She really had taken part in such a celebration, where she had raved against racism amongst the crowd of Afro-Brazilians, but she had been so drunk that night that she could not for the life of her remember whom she'd talked to. Turning her head but not her back, she gave a vague, reserved greeting. She hadn't yet caught Armando's eye. She lit a cigarette. The back table had broken out in a flurry of voices; she picked out a few words, variations on the term black, like *preto* and *negro*. It had been a year and a half since she and Roberto had broken up; but it seemed that in the eyes of

Lapa's black community, he was to remain her lover, in this world and the next. They adored Roberto... He was black, an orphan, an alcoholic, and "a famous actor"—if that's what one should call the leading man at *Ta Na Rua* Theater—who'd dropped anchor in the world of the whites and managed to stay afloat...

Özgür had gone to a lot of trouble to erase him from her memory; in fact, Roberto was the only person of the many she had met in Rio not to infiltrate her novel. He was a man made of dark, ominous clouds and lightning, bitter like poison hemlock; the term "psychopath" fit him like a glove. A "rape baby," to put it in his own words... His mother, who died when he was just two years old, had been a kept woman. The players at *Ta Na Rua* said that he was the only black person in Brazil who couldn't dance. He was short, puny, hardly attractive, but his lively eyes, which flashed like fireflies, darting from one object to the next, made him singularly endearing. Because they didn't share a language, their relationship had been based upon physical communication alone—the most violent of all forms of communication. Özgür's first months in Rio had been so painful, her loneliness amongst the aimless throngs so agonizing that she'd tried with all her might to wring some smidgen of love, affection, or something to take their place, out of this stark raving madman; a fool's errand, like squeezing oil out of a fly. For every gasp of pleasure cost her dearly, each paid for with multiple lashings of humiliation. In the blink of any eye the *gringa*, who held her body in no esteem, was easily duped and, utterly ignorant of the Byzantine games of desire, turned into a sex slave, the Middle Eastern beloved of a harem. Roberto had taken her by her gaunt shoulders and forced her into the dungeons of passion where she thrashed sweetly in the throes of death.

They'd run into one another countless times. Rio, the city that catches you in its net only to abandon you to a blind roll of fate's dice, brought the two of them together on numerous occasions. At parties, cinemas, concerts, and once even right in front of her own apartment... It was as if he were the dark refrain in her song of death. He seduced the *gringa* with his harsh gaze every time. Even after that night... Even after that night when he had squeezed her breasts and twisted her arms until she'd begged for mercy... "What could possibly keep me from doing evil in a city where murder goes unpunished? Anything goes in war." That's the slogan she'd had framed and hung on her conscience. The last time, they'd come face to face on the Santa Teresa bus, close to dawn, after the *Juninho* festival, a celebration of pagan origin. He'd scrutinized Özgür's inanimate face, a statue in marble, with undeceivable, sneering eyes, and given her a smile that stung like a knife wound. "You're so much stronger now. Rio helped you discover your secret weapons. But you're still as fragile as ever, too. You just can't quit chasing after that thing you fear the most, can you?"

What remained of Roberto, whom she'd locked away in a quarantine cell of her memory, was a feeling of having been soiled, a feeling that was like a permanent stain upon her being, and the hours she'd spent by herself on the second floor of the theater while she waited for him on those neverending rehearsal nights. Dances performed on a stage fraught with cracks, the sad echo of footsteps in an abandoned hall, black velvet curtains, rats the only audience... Rows and rows of costumes and masks on hangers... Theater was a world in which truth and lies were intertwined, where blatant fabrication was transformed into a living, breathing, vital reality all its own. An absolutely perfect metaphor for Rio, the city that never removes its mask, not even after carnival...

"Hey, *gringa*! Look here!"

There was no escape. Reluctantly, Özgür turned around.

"You know what? They're calling me a racist because I told them your lover was black. Do you think that makes me a racist?"

Özgür was caught off guard. To tell the truth, it was an unexpectedly prickly question. "No, why?" was all she could manage in response.

The woman started screaming at the top of her lungs.

"See there! Take that for an answer! I'm not racist at all. Even the *Turca* says so!"

This time a cacophony of voices rang out from the table, from which she was able to discern the words Turk and Turkey. She couldn't tell exactly what was going on, she only knew that a heated discussion about her was underway. She nervously puffed at her cigarette, exhaling noisily each time. "Damn it! If only I hadn't been such a cheapskate and just gone to Ernesto!" she thought.

"Hey *gringa*. Why you so quiet? This gal's so damn shy! Shoulda seen her when she first got here, fresh from Turkey... She'd go all red in the face even when she danced. She's opened up a bit now though. Hey, tell me, how do you say '*cinzeiro*' in Turkish?"

She felt her heart tighten in her chest. They'd pierced her emotional armor just like that. In the two years since she'd set foot in South America, no one, not her lovers, her colleagues, her students, her European friends, none of them had asked her a single question about her mother tongue. She welled up with gratitude, and resentment. And that miserable, ash-gray feeling of loneliness...

"*Küllük*. Ashtray is *küllük*."

The woman didn't listen to her response. She was having fun making the financially carefree *gringa*, little miss Snow White, dance to her tune. A rare opportunity to play first fiddle at the men's table.

"And how about '*mon amour*'?"

From the table boisterous laughter, amorous moans, and loud slurpy kissing sounds began to rain down upon Özgür. She was surrounded on all four sides; she meekly resigned herself to the role assigned to her, as always.

"*Sevgilim*."

"What? Say that again."

"SEV-Gİ-LİM. Now enough with the questions, please!" Then she yelled out: "Armando! A milk coffee... Please."

She turned her back to the hoopla that was gradually getting out of control and raised her shield to the outside world. She cringed, as if trying to make herself smaller, thicker, more compact. As if her bony shoulders were her only defense against this city which stuck a thorn in her heart every hour. She never had been brazen, quick-witted, or good with a comeback. Like all timid and open-hearted people, she was easily transformed into a plaything in the hands of those many times stupider than herself. She was, after all, a *gringa*; she didn't stand a chance against these tipplers, not with her stiff, slang-free Portuguese. As she reached for her cigarettes, she noticed that her hands were shaking. Before coming to Brazil, she thought that such a thing happened only to figures in novels or women on the verge of menopause. "Have I really been insulted, or can't I even take a little well-intentioned teasing anymore? I truly am at the end of my rope." She'd long forgotten all about her first cigarette, which was still burning away on its own in the ashtray.

Thankfully a doll-faced mulatto of twelve or thirteen walked into the New World, moving all attention away from Özgür. Like all girls of Rio her age, she wore a ton of make-up and was so scantily clad that it was mind-boggling. The purple lipstick on her thick lips reminded Özgür of damson plums. She swaggered into the bar like a female panther, tossing her hair violently about like a shawl on fire, looking ferociously determined to seduce any man who crossed her path. She displayed her breasts, which spilled out of her brassiere, and her lush, shapely hips with appalling recklessness and abandon, the same way greenhorn gangsters display their latest model pistols. This body, which had lost its innocence much too young, and which was cast about with the extravagance of a prodigal daughter squandering her inheritance, made Özgür—and probably Özgür alone—feel sad. Like all of the other mass-cloned women of Rio, the girl had internalized a desire that was not her own; she had become a mouthpiece for the lust for power, proclaiming loud and clear the insatiability of flesh, as dictated by this city. Like a puppet hanging by her strings, she was tangled in the binds of her sexuality, and there was no escape. When tourists who stormed Rio in quest of second-hand fantasies saw her, they immediately began fondling their wallets. Yet she wasn't a real professional, even if she did put her body up for sale, sometimes out of financial need, but most of the time just for the tiny thrill of it, or for a change... Like most girls from the *favela*, she was a daytime beauty. A violet mushrooming in the slums...

Like wolves having caught a whiff of blood, all of the waiters, except for the shy Armando, were watching the girl's hips as she made her way to the table of negroes. Her shorts, ripped here and there, stopped a few centimeters above her ass. She obviously was not used to restrictions such as underwear. "WANTED" was written on her tits in strawberry colored lipstick. Özgür couldn't help but laugh. "Of course you're WANTED, sweetheart. It's hardly the Hope diamond that you're peddling there, but it is the most WANTED thing in the world all the same."

She felt the slender shadow of Armando glide up next to her. A hand soft like that of a woman, afraid of inflicting damage, gently set her cup on the table. Özgür raised her eyes; they smiled at one another. The knowing, innocent smiles of confidants... Armando was a slightly hunchbacked, wiry mulatto; he had curly hair and long, black eyelashes. His face had the fine lines of a miniature, and it reflected a misery shut off to the outside world, a storm not yet calmed... Özgür sensed a trace of Middle Easterness in him; maybe one of the Syrians, *O Turco*, who had migrated to Latin America at the turn of the century, had tumbled in the hay with his ancestors.

She wrapped both hands around the glass and freed her mind of any thoughts. With a slight slurping sound—after all, there weren't any spectators around to make her observe the rules of etiquette—and rolling the cream on her tongue, she finished her drink in almost a single gulp. She was covered in sweat again, and had failed to quench her relentless thirst, but at least her stomach was settled. Finally, she was alone with her cigarettes and her loneliness.

Unlike the touristy bars of Copacabana, this place didn't contain the slightest hint of the tropics; no fishing nets, brightly colored parrots, seashells, naïve Bahia paintings, etc. On the wall, marked with long cracks running through its plaster, hung a Japanese miniature—a woman wandering in a cherry tree orchard with a placid smile on her face, and a slightly bewildered gaze, as she watched the insanity of the New World. And next to her was a Brazilian flag left over from the days of the World Cup. There was a globe, slightly squished on either side—probably symbolizing the world—with a pendant stuck in it that read "System" and "Progress." An extraordinary irony that could make Özgür laugh even after two years!

For a while she distracted herself with the fly that kept coming back for more of the tomato sauce stain that looked like a mosque with three minarets. She got a whiff of the scent of fresh coffee weaving its way amongst the tables. Should she have another cup? She took her green notebook out of her bag.

Whenever she wanted to take a profound look into her personal history, she had her last two years right there waiting for her. Woven, braided, varnished, tailored memories... Half-finished stories, first-person confessions, quotes...

Like fields of wheat, the Brazilians were blown this way and that by the winds of social events; Mother's Day, the death of Ayrton Senna...And then, after Valentine's Day, they got caught up in another instance of mass hysteria: the World Cup. Game days were declared national holidays; buses quit running and shops closed down after two in the afternoon. An entire country, everyone from nine to ninety, clad in yellow, wielding flags of all sizes and snatching up bugles, drums, tabors, whistles, rattles, etc., anything that could be used to make noise; hoarding fireworks, confetti, beer; groups of at least twenty people packed into houses, bars, restaurants, and concert halls equipped with massive television screens. Because watching the national games by one's self was considered to be one of the worst disasters that could possibly befall a human being, even I was barraged with invitations.

It was an early afternoon in July. The rain poured down, as if eager to tear the city asunder, to cleanse it of all its filth. There wasn't a soul on the streets. All transportation had come to a halt, the metal shutters were pulled down on all of the shops, and even the homeless had long ago escaped to whatever shelter they could find. The Russia game would be starting in half an hour. Meanwhile I was trying to make it home, the only place where I could take refuge from the imminent tumult.

I ran into him at the entrance to a movie theater in Cinelândia... He—I'll name him after I've described him—was lying in a puddle of mud several inches deep. Needle-sharp droplets of rain pierced his face. Though he had not yet crossed over the threshold to death, he had certainly drifted so far from the shores of life that there was no turning back. He was about to die of hunger. His body had betrayed his soul, expelling the last bite he'd had to eat. With his last ounce of strength he tried to reach his vomit—so that he could eat it once again.

Nobody paid any attention to him. A few stragglers scurried across the nearly empty square, rushing to make it in time for the game; after all, they were used to the many and varied performances of death. Only I stood there, motionless, under the rainstorm, my face drained to bone-white. It was as if I'd turned to stone. I could neither cry nor yell; a tight fist, a silent scream caught in my throat. I recalled a film I'd seen years ago. (Fiction versus reality! But to what degree can the former possibly save you from a one-on-one confrontation with the latter?) The American protagonist in the film was talking about the most dreadful hunger he had seen in his life, at a secluded hotel in the middle of the tropics: A native picking out the undigested pieces from amongst a pile of human feces... I was sick at my stomach for days, I didn't think that there could possibly be a more incisive description of hunger. But the naked reality of the streets of Rio was even more atrocious than the most atrocious of fictions. With a few blows of the hammer it had engraved a portrait of hunger into my mind.

I simply must tell, tell everyone about that man whom I encountered in Cinelândia half an hour before the start of the Brazil-Russia soccer match, that is, at a precisely definable point in time and space. (Whether they want to listen or not.) The price must be paid for that scream that got caught in my throat. I was cursed because I did nothing but stand there and watch him like that for several minutes, before continuing along my way. Because there was nothing to be done, because I didn't find a spoon and feed him his puke, because all of the kiosks were closed, and a biscuit would never have made it on time, because I didn't draw a pistol from my purse and put a quick end to his misery... What did I have to offer him? To deny him? I continued on my way, for I had charged myself with a mission. An excuse for postponing my own death...

Yet now, as I look at the letters I have lined up on the white piece

*of paper before me, I cannot see that man. I still lack the language to
express him. I am not strong enough, not vicious enough, not merciful
enough. I have not experienced enough hunger. Words cannot give him
back his life, but at least they can offer his name restitution: He was a
Human Being.*

She was suddenly overcome by an odd feeling, as if her own sentences had just done an about-face and had begun watching their
author. She grabbed her pen and struck a big X across the page.
Then she wrote a single sentence:

*"I write to show myself larger than I really am, because... I am so very,
very small."*

As she walked up to the cash register, a well-kept homeless woman
walked into The New World and, raising her voice every so slightly,
asked: "Anyone here want to buy me a meal?" Measured, polite,
kindly, like an abashed college student asking the other passengers if they have an extra bus ticket... There was no response; only
Özgür lowered her head in shame. "Thank you," the woman said,
bowing her head before making a silent exit, like an extra who had
successfully completed her insignificant role. The prostitute, who
had faced her share of adversity in life, yelled out from the table of
drunkards: "This isn't the Third World, you know—it's the Eighth
World! The Eighth!"

Özgür looked at the young man with the swollen legs, and
thought the woman was right. He was curled up like a fetus next
to one of the columns. He still wore that miraculous, pure, innocent look on his face. "This is an indigent people, clothed only
in its own luster... Making do with a love of life, of unknown
source... Yet what they call life is nothing but so much deception.
A banal gimmick passing for happiness."

She regretted not having said goodbye to Armando. She felt the kind of sentimentality generally reserved for prisoners spending their last day in jail; she wanted to leave behind good impressions of herself. She went back to The New World. Together with the mulatto girl, Armando and the other three waiters were standing next to the table of Negroes. Then, all at once, every single soul in the restaurant broke out in riotous laughter. "Who am I to think I have a monopoly on reality? I'm probably the last person in Rio who should be talking about happiness!" She managed to grab the attention of the busboy standing in front of the coffeemaker; she convinced the kid, who was looking at the WANTED hips like he was peeling a banana, to give her a paper cup full of milk. As she walked over to the kitten screaming in fear on the sidewalk opposite, she felt like a very, very old woman, who no longer had any expectations of life.

A TRAVELER IN THE STREETS OF RIO
—THE MULATTO WOMEN OF RIO

If there is any metropolis on this earth that belongs to mulatto women, it is Rio de Janeiro. A mulatto woman is an essential detail of any Rio photo taken at any time of the day, in any part of the city. The mulatto woman of the slums, with her curly hair, thick lips, full hips bursting out of her clothes, cross hanging from her neck... You can see her at the luncheonettes; she leans against the bar, drinking a beer and talking sassy; in front of the church she collects donations, a divine radiance emanating from her face... Children of all sizes hang onto her skirt at the supermarket as she lugs five pound bags of beans... On the sidewalks of Copacabana, she's put on her war paint, taken up her arms, and donned her net stockings, knee-high boots, leather g-strings, etc. On the covers of samba cassettes, half naked and crowned with parrot feathers taller than she is, she happily radiates big smiles and shakes her hips with all her might. On a dust-covered bus to the slums after nightfall—half dead after twelve hours of serving others, her eyes two dried-up wells—she eats her evening meal from a dinner bucket on her lap. More than anywhere else, though, you'll see her on the beach... Like a mermaid deposited upon the shores by the ocean waves... Her hair wet; lips smelling of coconut milk; a carelessly wrapped pareo; *munificent, easy-going, frisky hips; skin pampered by the sunrays' constant fondling... Contrary to popular belief, the mulatto women of Rio are not beautiful; that is, not according to Western standards. They're short, fat, stubby... But they are so utterly stunning, and they impose their attractiveness with such abandon that, in Rio, Woman equals mulatto.*

It is these women who attract the epicurean, pampered gringo to this city, where life is a fight to the death begun anew every morning of every day. It is they who make the gringo toss his money about like confetti... In the blink of an eye they transform this rat race of a third world metropolis into a tropical island. A fictional island existing only on tourist posters, full of golden beaches, palm trees, and seashells...

They walk with lithe, rhythmic steps, always, as if they are carrying bunches of bananas on their heads, or doing the samba in slow motion... Their heads in the clouds, calm, relaxed... They walk towards an invisible lover who stands waiting with open arms... An enchanting poem whispering in their ears, they smile at the passionate mirror in the emptiness. Infinitely aware of their femininity, they hold complete claim over their bodies, which have never belonged to them... Half drunk on their devastating power—a power as fleeting as a wildflower—they hold forth the promise of forbidden fruits more valuable than paradise itself.

On the plantations they learned of the terrible pillaging of the body... and of the body's value, and its price... The whip was their first teacher. They know that the world of worlds ferments in their hips, and that between their legs is concealed not the pen that writes history, but the wheel that extinguishes life. Though song lyrics make them sentimental and provoke genuine tears, and though they worship countless deities from soccer players to the good-hearted Jesus, and though they be doormats for one man to the next until they become wrinkled and frayed, they know. The body never forgets lessons taught by the whip.

The mulatto women of Rio are tough ladies. They have no qualms about giving the men they aspire to seduce long, lecherous looks, or about groping at tourists who gaze from blue, bleary, lashless eyes, or about peeing in the middle of the street. Their speech is loud and boisterous; they scuffle in hair-rending brawls; they defy the police, bus drivers, their bosses, and their husbands. Perhaps that is why they so stubbornly cling to their number one ranking in international violence and AIDS stastics. Because they've grown up three generations in a single room, their sexuality knows no shame or embarrassment. When they find themselves laden with a baby, the keepsake of a night of passion, before they've even hit fifteen, they feel neither rage nor sadness. It is as if every disappointment, every let-down, every child further fortifies their femininity. In this city, which does not allow them to be anything but women, they have remained, until the end, women. JUST-WOMEN.

The black-skinned, black-eyed, black-haired mulatto, doing the samba with death all her life... Its stygian, abysmal, permanent darkness is within her body. In her body only... Because she has no soul. It was taken from her long ago.

POINT ZERO

Let the dead bury the dead.
—The Bible

In Lapa, which is like an anthill teeming with homeless people, she wouldn't dare take her watch out of her purse, but she could tell it was around six o'clock. An evening full of distant shadows was well underway, and the streets had grown silent. It wasn't the silence that precedes a storm, but a silence containing a storm... A vague, somber sign of the night... In a little while, the world would close its aged eyes.

Özgür stood at the fork in the road glancing indecisively right and left. She had two choices: She could either walk down Gloria Avenue to the Flamengo Gulf, or she could go to Cinelândia Square, famous for its cinemas, night clubs, and open-air beer gardens. Cinelândia... The Land of Cinema...

A poster caught her eye: The dashing, renowned director with Broadway experience, Sergio Mancini, had adapted the MUSICAL OF THE YEAR: ROMEO AND JULIET, that "drama that never grows old," for the people of Rio—a people that thought of life itself as nothing but a musical. Dark-skinned Romeo of the *favela*, who nevertheless somehow managed to avoid a life of crime, and milk white, innocent Juliet of Ipanema... In this city, the allure of the flesh truly did supersede all class and racial differences; however, it did so to one exclusive end: satisfying the flesh. The other day she'd read a modern version of Romeo and Juliet on the crime pages of the newspaper. A bandito from the Turano *favela* convinced his lover (a university graduate, career woman, wealthy, etc.), a girl from Ipanema, who also happened to be involved with

the chief of another gang and had meanwhile managed to poach a
hefty amount of cocaine, to come to Turano; there, at the square
known as *Boca da Fuma* he subjected her to horrendous torture,
cutting off her hands, tongue, and ears, before killing her. The
incident was kept secret for months, until the Romeo of Turano
was killed in a gun battle. "Oh, love! That which makes the world
go round!" Özgür thought with a smirk as she looked over the
poster. And there it was, the name she had been searching for: Eli
Vitor de Santos. As Romeo...

The Land of Cinema was Eli's homeland. It was through the
dim and dank bars, gay clubs, and S&M shows—the ones without
neon lights or signs—of Cinelândia that he guided Özgür under
the faint glow of a flashlight. On Friday evenings they'd leave
their African dance course and have a glass of fresh coconut juice
at one of the luncheonettes before heading off into the night, its
darkness pierced only by the glint of blades. Bars with no women,
where no one paid Özgür any mind, full of smothering clouds
of cigarette and marijuana smoke, reeking of the sweaty
bodies of men where, disguised as desire, Azrael, the Angel
of Death, lurked, on the prowl for his next victim... Half-
naked negroes with shaved heads, bearing whips and chains;
transvestites in g-strings and net stockings, who could run rings
around any woman; show queens, barrels of hormones with fake
fingernails as long as carrots and hips as wide as pillows... Once,
Özgür nearly fainted while watching a queen, her belly hanging
down over her thighs, perform a show with dildos. Laughing
hysterically, Eli picked Özgür up and carried her outside. "Oh you
poor Turkish girl! That was obviously more than you can handle!"
(The queen was a high school history teacher by day; and the club,
which served up generous heaps of flesh at night, was a vegetar-
ian restaurant until ten.) On some nights Eli would get the urge
to "play normal," and on those nights he'd use the money he'd

managed to wrangle out of his lover to whisk Özgür off to the five star bars of Ipanema. They were always on each other's laps, getting frisky, half in fun, half in earnest, putting on dances that were risqué even for Rio.

But all of that came to an end on *Juninho* Night. The pagan festival, *Juninho* Night, when balloons full of candles and lanterns explode in the sky one after the other... "I'll be there in a bit. I'm heading out now," Eli had said on the telephone. Just how long had she waited for him in that pub? Maybe four, maybe five hours... There with those packs of degenerates, under a deluge of molestations, trying to ignore the propositions, ridicule, and glances that crawled over her body like slimy leeches... Finally, she'd dashed out to catch the last bus to Santa Teresa, been attacked by street kids at the square, survived an attempted robbery, and thrown the birthday present that she'd gotten for Eli—Oscar Wilde's *De Profundis*—into the trash. And then she'd run into Roberto.

She didn't head off to Cinelândia. She preferred the consummate rogues of Gloria to the inebriated masses storming the Sunday night Hollywood theaters, and the cokeheads to the young-tough mamas' boys. In the late evening hours, before night set in and the streets were left to the homosexuals, the square reminded her of Sundays during her early youth. Those suffocating years from which even the other side of the ocean offered no escape... Family picnics, sunflower seeds, black-and-white American TV shows, neverending homework assignments, restrictions, prohibitions, speeches, punishments... Rough amateur kisses, packs of Parliaments pinched from her mother, a pair of high-heeled boots, her first jazz records, and rambunctious afternoons at friends' houses... Mirrors bemused by her smiling rehearsals and the desperate chilliness of the gilded glass as it met her lips... Blood stains on her panties, the shame taking root in her adolescent body... Falling in love, and the death wish it awakened

within her... And a quest, always dim and melancholic... Life was
elsewhere, it belonged to others: those who were able to seize it.
The years during which a timorous girl, with unkempt hair and a
harsh gaze, became a woman... Slipping downhill into the world
of people... And now, she knew. Even if she fled all the way to
Amazonia, she would have to take her self with her. Together
with the weighty, moldy baggage of her past... If nothing else, this
much, at least, the trees of distant shores had taught her.

She sprinted down the first few hundred meters of Gloria
Avenue. This was a place well-acquainted with darkness, murder,
and destruction; it was full of prostitutes, muggers, AIDS-af-
flicted robbers armed with needles, garbage dumps, rundown
houses, dark and dank bachelors' pads, and motels with beds for
rent by the hour. At the top of the road which slithered its way up
to Santa Teresa like a cobra, and which no one dared to use, was
a fish restaurant. It offered fine Argentine wines and codfish and
was lit by candlelight only. All of the tables were for two. Özgür
had not yet found a knight to escort her through the two huge
torches at the door. Besides, by now she found flesh of all kinds
repulsive, and the thought of sticking her fork into a corpse made
her stomach churn. Just beyond the restaurant was Rio's most
famous sex hotel, offering all manner of equipment that one
might need for the act of copulation, from pianos to saunas, and
porn videos to whips, in rooms rented out for six or twelve hour
sessions. It was at this point, where the Flamengo Gulf began,
that Gloria suddenly transformed from a dirty, dusty wreck into a
broad, spacious, tree-lined avenue.

The streets were coming now to life. The impatient stirrings of
a tropical night about to break out of its cocoon... Özgür walked
into the emerging night, slowly, absorbing all the sounds, the
sights, and the smells... The warm, syrupy, humid air pressed
against her lips like a wet kiss; the last rays of the waning day

skipped along the sidewalk. Strewn along the street were rotten mangoes, papaya, bananas, jackfruit, coconut shells, and cassava roots, which looked like dried branches and which she used to mistake for firewood, left over from the Gloria street market that had ended hours before. Crates, beverages, a few trucks, and samba melodies all around... The closer she got to the gulf, the more stylish, more light-skinned, and more dispassionate the people. Here the orderly rows of Portuguese villas, huge apartment buildings surrounded by iron bars, air-conditioned shops, and palm trees slowly began; the quality of the luncheonettes gradually increased; in short, Rio began putting on its postcard costume. Two young men wearing t-shirts bearing the emblem of their workplace walked by her. They were listening to the game on a pocket radio turned up full blast. "Hey, Minas Cheese! Come hang with us if you're stag," they said to her, blowing a dense cloud of beer into her face. They were in a good mood; their team had won again this week; the company where they worked themselves to death for a hundred dollars a month had increased its market share; Brazil had won the World Cup for the fourth time. One night when she and Eli were walking to Cinelândia, they had taken refuge beneath this overpass to escape the rain that was coming down in buckets. They had waited, shivering, for nearly forty minutes before deciding that they couldn't get any wetter since they were already drenched and so began running beneath the razor-sharp drops. "No matter where I am in the world, I'll always think of Rio when it rains," Özgür had said.

The avenue began to narrow again after the overpass. The sea disappeared just like that, as if made to vanish by a magician's wand; as a result of Rio's unique topography, the traveler walking parallel to the shore suddenly found herself with her back to the gulf. And it was at this point, where she and the Guanabara Gulf parted ways, that she went down to the beach. She gazed upon the still waters for a long time, like a rider on horseback standing at the beginning of a vast desert. One of the countless Özgürs inside of her was still in love with the ocean, the sunset, adventure.

Far from any human activity, the ocean was calm and austere, withdrawn into its own world, lost deep in thought. It was as if the Guanabara Gulf were the door to eternity, with the sky so expansive, its beauty beyond words, as it stretched from the horizon into infinity. Sundown... The hour when life, in all of its magnificence and all of its misery, was cast in afterglow... In the tropics, an ending was never experienced as a conclusion, never awakened feelings of sadness. It was more like the first notes played by an ecstatic symphony; it made a worn-out, dilapidated, exhausted dream brand new, creating it all over again. A dainty net of light had been cast over the sky, like the gauze curtain of a temple; the clouds flashed, glimmering in gold and purple. A gigantic dark bird carrying the night in its swaddling clothes slowly spread its fire-tipped wings. A calm, pure, clear, immortal sky...

She turned around. She looked at the Blue Hill *favela*, a tiny freckle in the jungle shrouded in red mist, and at the iron Jesus trying to embrace the city with his puny arms. It was time she got back home, before night, making its sudden descent, took her by surprise once again.

A bum, his face covered in pockmarks, walked by her, talking to himself and hurling guffaws and expletives left and right. He was pushing a cart full of at least twenty dogs all tied up with laundry line. She ran into the man almost every Sunday. She pitied the dogs. Some of them barked with all their might, hoping to pierce the thick-skinned hearts of the people of Rio, while others howled and howled with the same fierce exuberance of their wolf ancestors. Most, however, passively bowed to their fate, just like the street people whose protein needs they met. She fixed her eyes upon a particular spot and stared, counting to twenty, an effective method she had developed to keep her from puking, or crying. Before she even realized it, she had begun praying. Everything she encountered was telling her that death made all dreams come true in this city; that here, death had found its very own nook of paradise.

She slowed down when she got to the Catete Police Station and quickly scoped out the area, her eyes moving at the speed of light, like those of a master thief. She once spent eight hours in that dirty pink wooden villa with its unkempt front yard overrun by weeds. They'd left her sitting there under the sun, hungry, thirsty, and without cigarettes; they'd held a gun to her head; they'd told her how they were going to break her fingers using something like a ping-pong racket. It was at the time when she'd just begun working at the Society for Protecting Street Children. While waiting at the bus stop, she'd heard someone cry out, "That's her! That's her!" A car had then come to a sudden halt right next to her and three civil police had leapt out, grabbed her by her legs and arms, and brought her to this spot. It was only hours later that she finally understood that all of it had been for the sake of wringing a thousand dollars out of her. But Özgür hadn't given in. In a country where concepts like justice, trial by law, and defense were considered nothing but encumbrances, she had not been deterred by those police, whose language she hardly understood; she had managed to get out of that sewage pit scot-free, without paying a cent—she didn't have any money anyway—for her freedom, or her fingers. The odd thing about it was that she felt no resentment towards the torturers, or that cotton-candy-sweet building (all police stations and barracks in Rio were painted in tones of pink). Every time she walked by it, she scanned the windows with an irrational longing, tried to figure out in which room she had been questioned, and felt a perverse desire to run into "her" policemen.

For some reason, she wondered if they would recognize her. After all, the Catete Police Station was one of very few buildings that held a memory for her in this foreign city.

The most vivid recollection she had was that of her companion in misfortune while in custody. He'd been locked onto a balcony the size of a bathtub, located directly beneath the noon sun. He'd crouched down on the sizzling stones, rolled up in a ball to protect his face from the rays. It was a long time before Özgür finally noticed the courtyard, which was partitioned into cages like a zoo, or the fat mulatto with the handlebar moustache there in his underwear. The man had raised his head and was looking at Özgür, like an old sailor gazing upon the stormy seas, never averting his glance, not for even a second... He was asking a profound, painful, quiet, infinite question of unknowable meaning. Özgür was wrapped up in her own predicament. She just stood there staring back at him. She looked at him with a fixed gaze reflecting nothing but her own emptiness, containing not a hint of compassion, attachment, any kind of message... Each of them had gotten lost in the depths of their own pain, there in the eyes of the other, until the police took the *bandito* in for questioning—maybe for torture, maybe to his death.

The process of destruction had begun, like everything in this city, at a dizzying speed; before she knew it, she had arrived at the point of no return. The wild seeds of doom had suddenly taken root in her soul. Over the coming months they would germinate, furtively, and, feeding on the hopelessness accumulating in her heart drop by drop, wax forth. Like trees that grow in the dark.

She had made it through her third week in Rio. (Only three weeks!) She had already fallen for the seductive call of Hades and made her first favela *journey, enrolled in an African dance course, learned the bus numbers, cigarette brands, and the simple present tense in Portuguese, come eye to eye with the Atlantic Ocean, discovered Queijo Minas, that distant relative of Turkish white cheese, and papaya juice, and gone to a dozen festas and met dozens of people. She'd even fallen in love and been dumped already. Her left index finger had been broken when it got stuck in an elevator door. A dentist on the street where she lived had been hit with a rain of bullets because he refused to hand over his watch.*

She was broke in those days, too, but she nevertheless continued to fritter her dollars away with the expectation of the salary she would secure on the day she finally managed to conquer the onerous bureaucracy of Brazil. She and her only friend, Deborah, went to jazz clubs, Ipanema bars playing bossa-nova, and Japanese restaurants almost every night. Deborah snubbed anything less than four stars. They worked at the same university, but it seemed that nothing in this world interested this nearly forty-year-old woman less than academia. It was in the realm of her various pleasures that her brilliance shined: Japanese cuisine, the sea, the sun, samba, erotic adventures, love… (Ah, love!) And she was also obsessed with astrology. Though nearly short enough to be considered a dwarf, she was a breathtakingly beautiful woman, with an hour-glass figure reminiscent of the Hollywood stars of bygone eras, red hair cascading down her back, a tiny but ever so regal nose, and sea blue eyes that shone like wet pebbles. In the full sense of the word—breathtaking. She had become a veritable virtuoso of seduction. She whet her attractiveness on a daily basis through a regular series of exercises, tests, and formidable challenges. Purring, cuddlesome, vicious; a catwoman who was a magnet for desire.

She was across from the former President's Palace, which had been converted into a Cultural Center. (On the morning of the military coup, the then-President of Brazil committed suicide, with a single bullet to the head, on this very spot.) She was at a pizzeria that was a cut above The New World. There were no stains on the red Formica tables; the waiters were not only polite but nimble, too; hollow, oily pastries had been replaced by pizzas bearing French names. There were at least forty different kinds of fruit juice written on the board that covered the wall from top to bottom. Tropical fruits, exorbitantly priced imported fruits like peaches and strawberries, Amazonian fruits with names reminiscent of those of slaughtered Indian chiefs: *Tamarindo, Cupuachu, Genipapo*. Because the people of Rio never deviated from the usual, nobody except for a few *über*-curious foreigners like Özgür ever tried the latter drinks. It was at just such a pizza joint that she had met Darren. The Englishman was trying to order a mushroom pizza using exaggerated arm and leg movements and, without realizing it, shouting, when he turned to the Turkish woman, who had just sweated blood trying to explain that she wanted a *mate* drink rather than cola, for help. He had mistaken her for a Brazilian, what with her curly hair, short stature, and half a dozen words of Portuguese… Darren was in Rio to make a documentary film about the murdering of street children. He was a missionary of the age of communication, dedicating his life to his work, that is, to the weepy-eyed voyeurism of the First World. Armed with a camera in one hand, dictionaries in the other, and a back pocket full of malaria pills and condoms, having had all his shots for everything from typhoid to yellow fever, he was constantly risking his neck on perilous journeys, dashing about from Nicaragua to Bosnia, from the deserts of Africa to the slums of Brazil.

Özgür knew well and good within three weeks time that she would never be able to make it on her own in the maelstroms of Rio. She was hoping a new love affair would soothe the fresh pain of having been left high and dry, though what she mistook for a desire to be consoled was really the boxer's anxiety as he sought to hang in the match after a walloping clout. The fact was, she had already gotten caught up in a current much stronger than herself, and now she was fated to be dragged along, smashing into one rocky shore after the next. The two strangers, besieged by the city's brutality, would inevitably draw closer, sailing towards one another with the force of the erotic winds blowing off of the beaches. But then, before the timid relationship of this Old World pair had a chance to bloom in the steamy climate of the tropics, Özgür would make another of her countless mistakes in this city; she would introduce Darren to Deborah. For the born and raised native of Rio, one night was all it took...

Deborah was going to take the tourists—breathless from dashing around the neon signs and Eroticas and Pussy Cats of Copacabana—to Santa Teresa. To a bar where all the customers sang in unison and accompanied the music with tambourines, tabor drums, and matchboxes, and where pairs danced amongst the cramped and wobbly tables... (This was Özgür's first encounter with Sobrenatural, and with Santa Teresa.) Where, later, Deborah would exhibit her art as if performing her rendition of a Paganini sonata. An impeccable composite of goddess and sparrow, joy and tenderness, attack and withdrawal... Sometimes dancing, sometimes singing *pagodes* in a slightly husky voice, with movements poached from Edith Piaf... And then proceeding to twist a napkin and explain the Mobius strip... Probably no one else on this earth could possibly make the word "Mobius" sound so titillating. (That's when Darren turned to Özgür and said, "Such a beautiful woman, and so intelligent as well! Unbelievable!" As if seeking confirmation from her that he had indeed made the right choice. Then he added: "Hey, you're a mathematician too, right?") Özgür desperately regretted never having had brains enough to explain the Mobius strip to a man before; wearing ratty jeans instead of a tight, bright red dress; not having pierced her ears or bought lipstick yet in her life; not being able to hold her tongue but instead waxing effusive on the matter of her "amorous adventure."

The truth was that, compared to Deborah's, her Middle Eastern
flirtation methods were ponderous, clumsy, and ludicrous, like
the war chariots of ancient history. Next to this beautiful, charming, skillful, fast, enchanting woman, she felt like the Abominable
Snowman in the Himalayas. She ran down a list of adjectives that
could be used to describe Deborah: coquettish, enticing, flighty...
(Much later she would use the same adjectives when describing
Rio.) Presenting a flawless image of that which she wanted to be:
A WOMAN.

And to rub salt into Özgür's wound, the couple at the next
table had been kissing non-stop, except for the occasional drink
and toilet break, as if they were partaking in some kind of couples
championship. And as if to spite Özgür... Like court jesters using
exaggeration to show reality in its purest form to the king. And a
weepy chorus piece played in the background, so appropriate to
the melodrama. Her stomach twisted in a cramp. They ended up
having to carry her to the car and quickly spirit her home.

*The sun was about to rise as she set her alarm clock for eight. Even
taking pity upon herself no longer provided solace. She was alone in
the five room mini-palace, as the owners had gone to São Paolo for
Easter. Like a tiger in a cage she wandered about amongst the heavy
couches draped in covers, mahogany coffee tables on slender legs, silver
candlesticks, religious paintings doused in blood from top to bottom,
Madonna curios, Spanish swords, duello pistols, books of absolutely no
interest to her, written in a language she didn't know—books on sailing, Italian cuisine, the Brazilian Constitution, etc. When she could
no longer stand the pain in her stomach, she would collapse onto the
Persian carpets and drive her fingernails into the couch covers to keep
herself from screaming. As if anyone would hear her if she did scream!
She was surrounded by arrogant, presumptuous objects all looking
down and sneering at her; even the mirrors derided her. An antique*

cuckoo clock sang out every hour, on the hour: "You idiot, you idiot!"
That pair of doves, D. and the other D., stood down in HER street
(neither the house nor the country was hers, but she claimed the street
as her own) chatting for about forty minutes, twittering like parrots,
their laughter soaring up to the fourth floor, in a conversation that
most likely did not include the Mobius strip, before they finally went
off to some unknown destination.

   Just as night was settling in, before Cleopatra of Rio made
her grand appearance, Özgür and Darren had agreed to meet on
Copacabana beach at ten the next morning. She knew he wouldn't
come, but she nevertheless woke up at the crack of dawn and prepared
to leave. She was undertaking once again that which an unkempt
woman newly arrived from a winter country and who is generally
careless about her appearance must do before putting on a bathing
suit; that meaningless, Sisyphean battle against bodily hair. She felt
exactly like the hairs that fell onto the newspaper she'd spread out on
the floor; natural, harmless, and for some reason, unwanted.

   Easter, an Easter when all clocks stopped, had begun thus. Nobody
showed up at Copacabana. Sure, half a million people crammed onto
the four kilometers of beach with their g-strings, pareos, guitars,
tabor drums, and bodies that shined as if they'd been deep-fried. But
nobody came for her...

   Easter had begun, and all clocks had stopped at the behest of the
evil will that reigned over the city. The alarm clock had performed
its final duty at eight o'clock, the derisive, talkative cuckoo birds had
suddenly retired to their nests, and the batteries in her wristwatch
had gone dead. She had not yet learned where she could buy watch
batteries, simple, infinitesimally small yet vital piece of information
though it was. The temperature had suddenly shot up to forty-two de-
grees. She couldn't get the air-conditioning to work. She was all alone
and shut up in a house that was like a cemetery, with a telephone as
still as a corpse. Four endless days, four abysmal nights... It was as

if she were already half-dead. Silence mounted a full assault; when the clocks stopped, so did time. Like a bug unable to break free of its cocoon, she was confined to pace within the confines of a single day. A warm, sticky cocoon gradually running out of oxygen... She'd begun having asthma attacks.

Sometimes she would reach the verge of insanity and throw herself out onto the broiling streets so that she could continue believing in the reality of the outside world. She'd walk up and down Copacabana Avenue, the only street in the city that she was familiar with. Like Rudolf Hess as the last remaining prisoner pacing back and forth in the courtyard of his prison. The heat rapidly devoured all of her energy. She couldn't read, or eat, or breathe. She felt her lungs were filled with warm phlegm. Every item of clothing she tried on was too heavy. Her lips were cracked from thirst, her urine was the color of mud. Blue lightning constantly struck before her lusterless eyes. All clocks had stopped and she was losing her mind; time went by so S-L-O-W-L-Y, so very S-L-O-W-L-Y. It spiraled and eddied and meandered, splitting and forking at deltas. Indecisive, forgetful minutes collapsing noisily on top of one another... Grains of sand dropping one by one... From life to death, from order to chaos, from life...

She ran into the mulatto woman of Copacabana on Holy Sunday. Their paths crossed at Point Zero. On that day, Jesus had completed his journey through the Land of the Dead and had decided to come back to Earth. Or a likeness of him, at least...

She'd left her apartment because of the piercing hunger that wracked her stomach. The only recent heartening development was her discovery of a Lebanese restaurant. She was fantasizing about the white cheese-stuffed pita and eggplant salad she would eat in the kiosk-restaurant consisting of four or five tables randomly scattered in front of a counter. The sole fantasy her paralyzed imagination was capable of producing... But she just couldn't seem to find the restaurant. She had recorded in her memory that it was located close to one of the bus stops; however, with characteristic carelessness, she had neglected to take note of the name of the stop. She walked around and around, nearly crawling, on the verge of passing out from hunger and heat. Then suddenly, on maybe her fourth trip in front of the same stop, she saw the mulatto woman. She was sitting with her back against an electric pole, her legs spread heedlessly in front of her, into the street where a constant stream of vehicles sped by. She was sleeping. She was barefoot and wore a dress that was so filthy its color was indistinguishable. Patches of grayish skin showed through her shorn head. She registered no reaction, even as the buses lapped at the soles of her feet, and the exhaust puffed at her face. What a deep slumber!

Özgür stopped a few steps away from her. There was something odd about the woman, or rather about the woman's color. Her face was a dirty yellow, what might be described as the color of beeswax; it was a very strange, very odd color belonging to no race. "Due to hunger, probably," was Özgür's original thought. Then all of a sudden, Özgür awoke, roused by the devil. Lightning that, rather than illuminating her mind, incinerated it... The woman was dead! She approached the woman with timid steps, ready to cut and run at any moment, trying to stifle her horror. She saw the deep wound, which looked like a hole drilled right into the point where her neck and skull met, and the dried blood covering her back. The woman had been killed! She looked around in desperation, wanting to ask for help. Cars, motorcycles, buses; they all carried indifferent people coming back from Easter service, or long, drawn-out meals, or the beach. Everyone was in their own little world; everyone had pulled down their blinds. The woman attracted less interest than an empty sack tossed in a corner. As if she were a horrendous, dirty yellow stain on the shiny, unblemished surface of life. A phlegmy gob of spit on the face of humanity!

Who could she possibly ask for help? She didn't even know the few measly sentences of Portuguese needed to ask someone for the address of the nearest police station. She was standing face to face with a murder

victim on the busiest street in the city in broad daylight, and she didn't
know what to do. She didn't even know where watch batteries were
sold in this damned city! "Let the dead bury the dead!"

Shattered, crumbled, ground to a pulp, closer to a state of nothing-
ness than she had ever been, she was running back to her sole refuge,
her five room mini-palace. Suddenly there it was, right in front of
her, like an oasis in the desert: the Lebanese restaurant. Without a
second thought, she walked in. She ordered a spinach-filled pastry,
eggplant salad, and a white cheese-stuffed pita. And an ice-cold
papaya juice… She felt nothing, absolutely nothing; only a vague,
insidious trembling had settled onto her lips. When she stabbed the
spinach pastry with her fork, a greasy, slimy clump of spinach flew
out of it. And at the moment, she thought she would vomit. Only at
that moment…

Nevertheless, despite her horrible feeling of queasiness, she ate
every last bit of her meal. The queasiness wouldn't cease for weeks;
it would continue for months, years. It would descend upon Rio like a
dirty yellow cloud. A greasy, slimy cloud offering no chance of escape.

The process of destruction had begun.

Now she, too, knew what every person who had arrived at Point
Zero knew: All of the corpses that a person encounters hit her in one
spot, her weakest: The corpse within.

She took a deep breath and laid her pen down on the table. Her
eyes were still on the green notebook, still stuck on her own past.
She had finished her novel. There was nothing left that she wanted
to tell the world. She'd described her hell down to the very last detail. She'd reached the last station in the labyrinth of reality where
all roads led to the same blind spot. She'd been tortured, and felt
as if she had shriveled to half her size; but at the same time, she
felt as if she'd grown. She had exited the process of destruction;
she had captured it for eternity within strict confines, like a bug

buried alive in amber. She had transformed it into an object that she could gaze upon in amazement whenever she pleased.

Noticing that an eerie silence had suddenly descended upon the restaurant, she raised her head. She was perplexed. She couldn't tell which of the two universes in which she found herself was more real. All of the customers had grown deathly silent, and were staring at the nearly two-meters-tall, fear-inspiring, burly man at the entrance, like an orchestra focused upon the conductor's wand. He was well-kept, but his clothes looked like they belonged to someone else. He had a lopsided cap on his head three of four sizes too small, and held a huge stack of paper. His gaze slid over the objects of his focus like butter. "It's like there's a well in the center of his eyes," Özgür thought to herself. "As if he's just finished reading the Book of the Dead, and just fully understood its meaning." She recalled de Oliveira.

The giant carefully looked at every single person in the room one by one, like a sultan scrutinizing his harem, before deciding upon Özgür. He spat a few words at her out of the corner of his mouth. A walloping curse or threat... He walked up to her, his awkward movements seemingly beyond his mental control, more like a gorilla than a man. Bumping into this and that, letting paper fall right and left... He stopped in front of Özgür's table, like a dark, black mountain.

"So you don't want to talk to me, huh?"

She quickly crammed her notebook into her purse. She had to win some time, to give the madman an answer that would get him out of her hair. Somehow all the lunatics ended up at her doorstep! Should she say that she doesn't speak Portuguese? It's never wise to make it obvious that you're a foreigner in Rio. Unable to decide what to do next, she raised her eyes and looked up at the man, simply letting events take their course. Just like that, the man attacked. Not Özgür, but the table right next to her, where a young man in worker's overalls sat by himself... He snatched the last slice of pizza from the young man's plate. He bit into it voraciously, angrily, vengefully. It was as if he sought to remind the world, which had tormented him so much, for so long, of its place; to prove that, despite all of its fat, its sauce, its fancy French names, he would rip humanity to shreds between his canines, at any moment he pleased... He'd downed half a slice in a single bite. He grimaced with revulsion. Even more agile and furious than before, in a single, grandiose motion he flung the remaining pizza back onto the plate. You could hear a pin drop; everyone, including the waiters, stood as if hypnotized. With the same swift, mechanical steps, like a jack-in-the-box leaping off its springs, he walked to the counter, grabbed the ketchup and nearly emptied out the entire bottle. And then he gulped down that poor last half slice, which now looked like a cormorant drowning in a sea of blood, and dashed out. He disappeared as fast as he had appeared, leaving behind reams of Methodist church bulletins, and the dark shadow of his anger...

Deathly silence continued to reign in the restaurant for some time, as if there was nothing left to say. Özgür was watching the young man who'd just had his last piece of pizza stolen. He was a little shocked, and a little hurt. Like all victims, he asked, "Why me?" He resented being watched, and by a woman to boot, while in such a pitiable state; he turned his eyes towards the street and put a smile on his face. As the little shop of horrors slowly livened back up; as the jokes and commentary and teasing commenced once again; as the customers went back to scarfing down their mushroom pizzas, gulping down their tap beers, and engaging in small talk; and as life returned to its familiar, common, safe state, like a branch springing back after it's been stretched as far as it can go; with what seemed like an almost supernatural willpower he continued to keep that smile tight on his lips. "A cross between the *Mona Lisa* and the cat in *Alice in Wonderland*," thought Özgür. She ordered a papaya juice and wrote her final sentences in the green notebook.

The equation for chaos is really very simple. Life = life. Death = death. Nevertheless each of us seeks to form our own equation and make the world equivalent to it. What vanity!

There is nothing in the real world deep enough to contain what's inside of you; but you, too, with your life, your death, and all of your dreams, are no larger than a hollow dot in the awful eternity of reality.

It was dark when she went outside. Another Sunday night in the tropics had begun. Rio de Janeiro was perhaps the only city in the world not to have fallen prey to the melancholy of Sundays. The *Cariocas* couldn't stand loneliness, silence, or sadness, not for a second. But still, but still... Sunday nights were always terrifying for a foreigner.

In a little while the streets would fill up with people feeling brand new after a cold shower, wearing fresh make-up, invigorated by nocturnal hopes. A mad rush for the *Domingueiras*, clubs, bars, restaurants, and beach concerts was about to get underway. From amongst the infinite available choices, everyone would choose a nook, a rhythm just right for themselves. *Samba, axé, bossa-nova, tango*, jazz... The flat broke would park their chaise-longues in front of the luncheonettes and turn their boom boxes up full blast. You could dance in any doorway, make love in any secluded corner. Even the street people could find a melody to hold on to. In the velvety night, death would dissolve, like a handful of powder paint thrown into water, and imprint its invisible signature on the night. Letters of lust that would be sent, naked, without envelopes of love. The people of the city would hoard everything they could get their hands on to fill the time until dawn. They would build a massive stack of crates of beer, bottles of *cachaça*, reams of songs, and lovers of various shades and tones, to defend themselves against the onslaught of loneliness. Özgür had been hoarding for months, too. She had bought pack after pack of ciga-rettes, lined up her pens, put her memories in order, and placed them on a conveyor belt to transform them into sentences. For months she had grasped tightly onto her pen, just like an acrobat walking the tightrope holds onto his balancing cane. Every night, without exception, she had sharpened her imagination with the determination of a knight girding his weapons; placing letter on top of letter, sentence on top of sentence, pain on top of pain, until, finally, she had built a fortress. A fortress whose secret weapon would be revealed at the first cyclone of reality...

A TRAVELER IN THE STREETS OF RIO
— NIGHT

The black velvet glove was slowly closing in on the ruby that sparkled on the horizon. The tropical night, capable of penetrating even a diamond... Like a wet tongue it licks the body, seeps through all the cracks and into the tissue; and there, deep down inside, it finds its rhythm. The night, reverberating in each pulsation...

The traveler would get caught up in the call of the streets, in its exquisite and unbearable lightness... She would latch on to one of the caravans en route to the land of the night. To lose herself in a sound, to find herself in a frenzy, to taste the most poisonous of passions. The sound of drums from afar; tom-toms, atabaques, marimbas, pandeiros... *She would arrive at the giant bonfire in the immense desert of loneliness. She, too, would join the crowds that danced hysterically. Divorced from her chains, ecstatic, cursed with pleasure... Those dancing desperately, so that their combined fires might illuminate the night surrounding them, and the night within them... To the same rhythm, in the same desert, on the same night... Those descending into the depths of nothingness, in step, hand-in-hand, shoulder to shoulder... The Great Secret was there, right there at that blind spot: Life is a dream seen between two blinks of the eye. A dream, that's all...*

"Screams, drums, dance, dance, dance, dance!"

AND
THE FIREWORKS EXPLODE!

Each person's destiny is personal
only insofar as it resembles that which exists in his memory.
—Eduardo Mallea

She was on the broad square between the former Presidential palace and the dark alleys leading up to the Blue Hill *favela*. The evening breeze blowing in from the ocean had loosened the iron collar around her throat. The last spectacles of the day were gradually being erased beneath the city lights and quietly retiring from the streets to make way for the night. Peddlers selling semi-precious stones, zodiac necklaces, toucan, hummingbird, and parrot figurines, and secondhand books were gathering up their stands; kiosk workers were filling up their coffee pots and rolling out kegs of beer for the thirsty travelers journeying through a vast darkness; street children were devouring the last wafers and candy on their display trays and, holding tightly onto their meager earnings, heading off in search of their mothers for dinner. Buses coming back from the beaches were packed full of salt-scented travelers with wet hair. Their bodies made languorous by all of the rays they absorbed, they had lain about like empty sacks, with sandy sandals, towels, and *pareos* strewn around them. A dapper crowd in front of the Cultural Center was waiting to enter the cinema for the 7:30 p.m. showing, with candy popcorn, cola, and cashews in hand. Özgür glanced over the posters. The cinema in the city center was the only place to watch decent movies. And showing that day: Bram Stoker's *Dracula*.

A boy of around fifteen or sixteen strutted by in what could only be described as a war dance. His hair cut to the latest fashion, like a rooster's crest, a pale orange t-shirt with a fish design

on it, American tennis shoes, and shorts with an emblem reading
"Child of Rio"... Everything about the guy just screamed, "I'm a
favelado, I'm fond of cocaine and cola. One of these days I'm going
to be one helluva gunslinger"... A melody ran through her head.
"*Ele era um bandito*..." The words pierced her heart once again; just
like when she'd heard them sung by the throaty-voiced man in
Santa Teresa that afternoon. Her eyes welled up with tears. It was
as if in a single, acute thrust, all of the pain, the disappointment,
all of the blows she'd been dealt in the past had become lodged in
a tiny spot of her heart, no larger than the eye of a needle. She'd
had enough; enough of clinging to life, of defending herself, of
taking slap after slap to the face...

"He was a bandit, but he was a good guy." Those dreadful
Sunday night migrations... They were long, excruciatingly long,
a thick residue, a clotted darkness... Clasping her pen, she wrote,
for writing was the only thing that made the night bearable. For
just as a soldier is acutely familiar with fear, and an acrobat is
intimately acquainted with her body, so, too, is the vagabond's
knowledge of loneliness profound. Especially a traveler in the
streets of Rio! A harborless voyager in the tropics... "What business do you have over there in that city anyway?" her mother
had asked, in a concerned, winter-scented voice of the northern
hemisphere. "Why haven't you come back yet?"

Her fingers went to the bulge in her purse, to the notebook,
its faint pulsations from beneath the worn leather revealing it
to be alive. "Even if I have wasted two long years, at least I've
written a book. It may not be of use to anyone, or save anyone from anything. They're just phenomena that I've selected
to replace reality, lies that lick my wounds... A few glimmering
twitches in an ocean of darkness. Tremulous, plain, enchanted...
I wrote, because I could find no other cover, no other protection
against death in this city which puts a value on human life of ten

to four hundred dollars per head. Now I am alone with my own hunchbacked child, but I'm even lonelier than before."

Eli suddenly appeared at the door to the pizzeria that was the birthplace of Point Zero, like Lazarus rising from the dead. He was going to the Cultural Center, his posture rigid like that of an Indian warrior, his stride unmistakably singular. When he walked, it was as if he danced to a magnificent rhythm that only he could hear... As if life were a *capoeira* dancer wielding his knife, but Eli had long ago learned how to protect himself from the attacks of his extremely agile, cunning, masterful rival. In the blink of an eye Özgür dashed into an alley and disappeared into the night, just seconds before they would have come face to face.

Eli was the sole photograph of Brazil—that cursed, riddled mass of a country—not splattered with blood. The sole name that kept her from striking a vitriolic X over an interminable list. Yet he was the veritable offspring of violence. He was born in the Africa of South America, the former slave port, seven-gated Salvador. "I don't remember my mother; she died before I'd even started crawling. And she probably has no recollection of my father," he'd explained, punctuating the ends of his sentences with the acrid, wry, touching smile he used in lieu of periods. "I was five the first time I was raped. When they rescued me from the clutches of my uncle and four of his friends, they had to give me stitches to keep me from bleeding to death. Even on my mouth... That day's been erased from my memory, but I still remember my uncle. Like they say, you know, you carry your first love with you for the rest of your life." His starkest memories of his childhood, a childhood which he describes as "a coal black stone that's still stuck in my throat," are the nights he spent in a wretched orphanage trying to fight off sleep... A broken bottom dog, he was beaten with iron rods every morning until the age of fourteen because he wet his bed. The hunger that was engraved somewhere even deeper than his memory, into his very body; the rapes, of which he became the perpetrator once his muscles were sufficiently developed; warm, ocean-scented rains slipping in through the broken windows of the dormitory; the wind bearing fog whistles, the chiming of bells, the beckoning call of distant shores... He became acquainted with the opposite sex at the age of eighteen; he had studied it like a European biologist studies Amazonian monkeys, but in it he failed to find any trace of his world. After so many Brazilian women, who were as clingy as stinging nettles and saw this black-skinned Hercules' homosexuality as a horrible waste, or even worse, as an insult, the introverted, frail Özgür, that *gringa* from distant shores, was a safe harbor.

They had met in the African Dance course in Flamengo. When she first set foot in the dance studio, she had progressed on wobbly knees before the gaze of the troupe, all of them professional dancers—and all of them black, and all of them gay—as their gaze turned her blood to vapor. (And they yelled out things like: "Another whitey who wants to dance like the black folk!"... "First she's gotta get fucked by a nigger, man!"... "Ouch, stop! That hurts!") She'd taken refuge behind the only person who smiled at her. And that's how she learned jazz dance, African rituals, *Candomblé*... And that sole secret of the body, to which only the black continent is privy: rhythm... Keeping her eyes riveted upon Eli's muscular back, imitating his incredibly elastic movements, simulating his dance, which gave each and every beat of the drum its due... They were the most intriguing pair in the class. A coal black *Candomblé* dancer with the body of a Greek god, and the skeleton-like, ivory white ballerina. The harmony that developed between them over time was nothing less than extraordinary. Even the haughty troupe had begun to treat her decently, despite her three deadly sins of being white, a woman, and a *gringa*. "There's only one way to dance in *Candomblé*," Eli had explained. "No inhibitions; you can't hold back; you can't hide anything. You have to dance like you're going to die, not tomorrow, and not in forty years, but right now—as soon as the music stops."

She had clung to Eli, exhilarated at finally having found someone to whom she could direct her love without danger. And Eli had clung back... Theirs was a relationship free of any kind of demand, tyranny, or bargaining. It bore the kind of spontaneity seen only in friendships between children. Full of purity and innocence, characteristics that were so agonizingly absent in Rio... Actually, Özgür didn't believe much in lofty words like "innocence." And she couldn't explain what purity meant either. The love she felt for Eli was definitely not non-sexual. To the contrary, she desired him so ardently, he made her quiver like a leaf caught in a storm. But still... But still, when she lay down on Eli's twin bed and rested her head on his chest, she felt that she was finally there, in her lost paradise, though she did not believe in the existence of it, and she had no idea what it was like.

Eli had seduced the dashing, renowned director, Sergio Mancini, with the Broadway experience; first, he had acquiesced to the whims of the sixty-something hedonistic man and took on the leading role in his sado-masochistic fantasies. And thus he managed to snatch the role of Romeo in the "Musical of the Year." Özgür now followed his dizzying ascent in the entertainment world via the newspaper only. The combined forces of the grizzled wolf's jealousy and Eli's savvy for survival, a trait he acquired at the tender age of five, immediately pushed Özgür out of the picture.

Juninho night, the pagan celebration, when a series of balloons full of candles and lanterns explodes in the sky one after the other... She'd waited at that awful pub in Cinelândia until the last bus to Santa Teresa. She'd thrown *De Profundis* into the trash and she'd run into Roberto. "You just can't quit chasing after that thing you fear the most, can you?" Roberto had said to her.

She hadn't called Eli again. She had written him, inscribed him onto the page. At the time, she likened her pain to that of a mother who's lost her son. But then she'd never had a child of her own. The only thing she had comparable to maternal love was her feelings towards *The City in Crimson Cloak*. But now she missed the Eli that she had written about in her novel, even more than she missed the real Eli. Dear Eli! Eli, who danced as if he would die when the music stopped, as if he had already died many deaths, but who learned to survive at the age of five! *Lama sabakhtani*?

A street lamp at the beginning of the path up to the *favela* came on early, illuminating the man in the leather jacket who stood there like a granite statue. Their eyes met. He looked Özgür over from her forehead down to her heels, with a gaze that slid down her like slimy snails. As if she were a tiny, foul-smelling bug standing before him. His face, blackened with the soot of an internal flame, was as bereft of life as that of a zombie. Warning lights went off in Özgür's brain. She had never seen such emptiness, such a void of meaning. "This man must not have a soul at all. A murderer... A murderer who kills, not for money or pleasure, but as a form of existence, a way of expressing himself. It's like he's jumped right out of the pages of *The City in Crimson Cloak*." She relaxed when she realized that the man wasn't paying any attention to her; he was watching the trucks climbing up the Blue Hill. He was probably a policeman, most likely a civil policeman from the Catete Police Headquarters.

FIREWORKS! Özgür was caught in the middle of a bombardment, and stood frozen on the sidewalk which shook with each terrifying explosion. She had forgotten where she was, where she was going, who she was even. Stark blue, phosphorescent flames suffused her consciousness. In a flash the fireworks surging from the Blue Hill *favela* had filled the dark sky with colorful comets, gushing springs of sparks, lotus flowers ablaze, and sparkling stones that poured down like bursting rosary beads. They were soaring towards the zenith of the endless void, and plunging into the deepest depths of the night, heading full speed into their demise, leaving twinkling traces of themselves behind. Straight to that moment when a powder-filled rocket gives birth to a fantastically beautiful universe, turns pumpkins into carriages and killers into angels, creates a land of fairytales out of a city in crimson cloak... To the miracle where the music of the Black Orpheus drowns out all of the moans, wails, cries of the earth... At that very moment, Özgür saw an imaginary mask shining in the nothingness, breathing.

By the time the cocaine-laden trucks reached the top of the Blue Hill, she had arrived at a wholly unexpected, traumatic illumination. The fireworks had drawn a portrait of the darkness with the quivering, magical traces of their demise, but at the same time they had catapulted Özgür into the past. Like a scream that both beckons the night and rips it to shreds. Özgür had understood that she was in love with Rio de Janeiro, where the word love perishes before it is even spoken. And that her fate had been intertwined with this city of cliffs ever since she first saw that boisterously-colored freak of a postcard... The city of cliffs, carcasses, and eagles... Rio was razor-sharp raindrops; the Santa Teresa bus with all the drunkards and muggers singing in chorus; the maddening cacophony of the carnival drums... It was that melancholy voice of the black man which had swept her off her feet from the very first day, and kind-hearted bandits; Eduardo's gifts; the mango trees of the ballet school with monkeys leaping from their branches; shells tintinnabulating to the breeze coming in from the valley... Eli's smile on that first day, a smile which would never be erased... the Guanabara Gulf, hiding the terrifying laughter of the ocean... The jungle, forever lunging forth in its interminable thirst for light, which had woven its branches in a firm embrace of her heart... She had loved the dangerous, hellish, melancholy tropics.

It was a love that existed for her alone; destitute, wounded, unconscious, so near to insanity, laden with revulsion and hate—a love fated to seek out its own annihilation. Like a flower fading in a shop window, poisoned before it could reach anyone, sullied in the most human way possible.

Death had confronted her at every corner; a fat, gluttonous, fickle death had infiltrated every word she wrote. Yet it was something else that she had tried to capture in those dark labyrinths. What she had sought in the veiled gazes of street people, behind the carnival masks, in the miserable *favelas*... The body's desperate desire for life, older and stronger than words... That was what had confronted her every day, every moment, pacing up and down on the streets like a sleepwalker... The rhythm beating at the heart of the city in crimson cloak, climbing up from the blazing sidewalks and wriggling its way into the body, was the rhythm created on the dirt floors of huts by slaves who had bowed down to the whip for centuries. It was the Black Orpheus who, when night fell and his body belonged to him alone, began to sing his melancholy tune. She had heard his melodies, had sensed them vaguely, had carried them within her; but she had failed to put them into words.

She had written *The City in Crimson Cloak*, and won her personal victory against death. Her trivial, insolent, clumsy, deceptive victory... Like a god seeing his likeness in the imperfect universe of his own creation, it was only now that she finally understood. She had never been able to love life, to love just for the sake of life. And she had never come to terms with it; but in the end, when she opened her eyes at Point Zero, she was able to bless it.

The street, with its mass of sacks and boxes and trash cans, was a car cemetery. Cars stripped of their motors, headlights, and tires had been rolled onto the sidewalks like so many torture victims. Chevrolets and Dodges from the 1960s... A Buick, its toothless mouth smiling like a corpse, its eyes gouged out... A half-burnt, aluminum skeleton... (Özgür couldn't tell what make it was, but its rear license plate was still in place.) She got a whiff of burning firewood which enveloped the street like a cloud rising from the underworld. She felt the warmth absorbed by the asphalt spread through her body as she walked haphazardly amongst the strewn nails, bolts, hoods, broken glass, and puddles of oil. A warehouse blew a breath of chilly air at her face. There was something about this street that seemed so familiar to her. Its scent, maybe... Her father used to wear the scent of the factory, the machines, the cables where he worked when he came home. In Özgür's eyes, it was a huge, masculine, confidence-inspiring world where only big and important work was done. Why hadn't she written even a single letter in months, since she'd begun writing her novel? Why hadn't she called Eli, not even once? Maybe she had preferred preserving the void within and writing him to the real Eli.

The singular exhilaration triggered by the fireworks was extinguished as quickly as a balloon punctured by a needle. The moment she reached the heart of reality, that she captured eternity, it had already slipped through her fingers. It had once again donned its veil of lifestyles, symbols, and concepts. Maybe trite lyrics, melancholy singers, drums, and fireworks were its unappreciated guides... "I played Anne Frank again. Mine is the crybaby sentimentality of migrants. When our loneliness becomes too painful, we transfer it from vessel to vessel, attributing such profundity to life, which is, in reality, so utterly meaningless!" She was obsessing about the technical details of her novel. For example, the first-person sections that she was couldn't decide whether to integrate into her novel or not. And she didn't know where to put the *Point Zero* chapter either. At this point, what she had constructed was more fragile than a house of cards. One mistake, and it was bound to collapse. She filed a footnote in the corner of her mind: "*Hanabi*, which means firework in Japanese, is the combination of *Hani* and *Bi*; that is Fire, which symbolizes death, and Flower, which symbolizes life..."

"Hey, give me your purse, or I'll slit your throat!"

She raised her eyes from the ground, bewildered like a patient aroused from slumber. She couldn't understand why she was being disturbed.

"Hey, you! I'm talkin' to you. Give me your purse!"

The young woman in front of her was a plump, extremely short mulatto, barely reaching Özgür's chin. Her dark brown skin gleamed beneath the light of the street lamp, and she had large, phosphorescent teeth. Her eyes were like those of a squirrel, and seemed slightly crossed. She was eighteen at the most, but her face had become aged before it had even shed the pimples of adolescence. She was wearing a bright pink blouse. "What an ominous color!" Özgür thought. She hated pink.

"No, dear. I certainly WILL NOT give you my purse," Özgür heard a voice say; but neither the ghoulish voice nor the words came from her.

"Give it to me or I'll slit your throat."

She slung the broken bottle in her hand in a slipshod, half-hearted motion. For a brief moment the dust raised by the wind flickered, drawing a shiny arc in the air. The threat she posed was such a showpiece that Özgür immediately sensed she was an amateur. From her body, Özgür could clearly read the fear that she tried to conceal beneath her poker face. A shot of courage borrowed by someone determined to act determined... She felt a pang of sympathy, and considered sharing everything she had with the girl. She even felt bad that all she had left was a few measly *reais*. For a moment, both of them paused. They didn't know how to go on. After a few seconds that seemed to last centuries, the young woman repeated her previous line, probably because she could think of nothing better.

"I'm telling you, give me your purse! Capiche?"

Suddenly, her eyes flared up. No matter how much her mind may have been dulled by hunger and beatings, she had been living on the streets of Rio for years. She was as cunning as a game animal that had been cornered time and time again. Moreover, she was a keen judge of character as well. She immediately discerned that the scrawny, haggard, absent-minded woman before her was a foreigner.

"Dollars! Dollars! Understand?" she said in English.

"I don't have any dollars, sweetie," Özgür said in suddenly fluent Portuguese. The truth is, she really couldn't stand being mistaken for a tourist.

"I'm gonna slit your throat!"

This time she swung the bottle with more aplomb, and the dust flickered once again. Having discerned that her victim was a foreigner had boosted her self-confidence and intensified her hatred. An arrogant smirk settled onto her face. Özgür stared at the woman's ample breasts gushing out of her revealing pink blouse. Due to their height difference, she could even pick out the woman's nipples. They were the most attractive pair of breasts she had seen in her entire life. They stood upright, as if swollen with milk, robust, luscious. She felt somehow ashamed of her own iron-board flat body. She looked at the girl's shoulders, which were so muscular it almost made her seem like she didn't have a neck; at her arms thick like those of a butcher; and at her stomach that strained at her zipper. She certainly didn't look like someone who was going hungry. Especially in comparison to Özgür...

The sky was lit up once again by the last few fireworks; stragglers who had missed the real show. Suddenly, Özgür believed herself to be in a musical. As if, in a little while, she and the girl would link arms and sing a few chirpy songs together; as if they would spin and skip and turn a few flamboyant figures, dancing and waving their shiny bottles amongst the junked cars. A Rio adaptation of *West Side Story*!

The rookie outlaw had misinterpreted the look in Özgür's eyes; she thought that she was trying to gauge her opponent in the overture of what would be a fight to the death. She tightened her grip on her weapon. All of the muscles in her body grew taut, making it seem as if she'd suddenly undergone a growth spurt; an ugly expression spread over her face. "I-need-to-get-my-shit-together-need-to-get-it-together-gotta-do-something-now." The words were running through Özgür's head fitfully like Morse code. Those brazen breasts sprawled out before her eyes were distracting her. Out of nowhere she'd become the lead actress in a cheap melodrama. Yet she herself felt like a spectator who, sick and tired of melodramas, had been forcefully dragged to the theater. She was both there and not. Just like in nightmares, she watched the person whom she knew was herself progress step by step to an inevitable end, but without being able to intervene.

"Dollars, *gringa*, dollars!"

She flinched violently as if she'd received a whiplash to the back. The word *gringa* had wrenched her out of her odd state of intoxication. The bird-brained adolescent with the bovine boobs thought she was a tourist, and couldn't tell that she lived in a state of semi-starvation. Did she not see her tattered purse and jeans shreded at the knees? How could she possibly not see that Özgür was an advocate of the street people, that she was a champion of the victims, the downtrodden, the consummate losers! She was not a tourist, but a forsaken vagabond. The sword was finally out of the sheath. Özgür made her move. She grabbed a broken bottle she'd noticed lying next to the sidewalk. *GRINGA!* She nearly screamed, out of spite, revolt, rage.

"Now let's see you come and get the bag, huh? If you can! My name is not *gringa*! You hear me? I am not *GRINGA!*"

She took short, strained breaths, as if she were having an asthma attack. Her eyes were narrowed and her lips stretched tightly, revealing her bottom teeth. Now she, too, wore the same expression that she'd observed on the mulatto's face a short while before. At that moment, it did not occur to her that she could die, or be killed. She had completely forgotten the concept of death, which had twined around her like ivy throughout her life. She was in a trance that bordered upon insanity. Across from her was a dark brown, misshapen, soft throat, its jugular visibly pulsating; that was all. That, and the ominous breasts spilling out of that blouse...

The young woman's face was as silent as stone. Only her eyes revealed, for a fleeting second, a vague surprise. Her eyes were fixed upon... No, not Özgür, but something behind her. Gradually approaching footsteps... One-two-three... five steps. Like the footsteps that a death row inmate waiting in his execution cell hears at dawn... Özgür counted five steps in the deafening noise, as if an entire city were collapsing at her very ears. Or maybe the fireworks had gone off again. A steel hand seized her heart, and with a terrible force pushed it down, towards her stomach. A click. The inevitable, lethal swish of a bullet sliding into the barrel. An irreversible, merciless reality too intense to deny... And she thought she heard a whistling sound, too. That odd whistling sound that she heard when walking down Santa Teresa, and which resembled the sound of a humongous bird spreading its wings... The man with the murderous face! Of course, there were two of them! The most popular mugging method in Rio! How she'd been duped! She'd fallen into a trap which even the most inexperienced tourist would not fall. She felt something warm run down her legs, which at that moment, felt like melting butter. For the first time in her life, she was peeing her pants.

"It's not over yet. I still have a chance. I'll toss away the bottle. No, I'll lay it down, slowly. No! First, I'll tell them that I surrender, and then I'll put it down. Whatever you do, don't make any sudden movements! Do not upset them! Everything has to happen slowly. C'mon now, gather your strength and talk! TALK!"

Silence... Her tongue was tied in a taut knot; not a single word came out of her mouth. The bottle slipped from Özgür's hand and shattered on her foot, but she was oblivious to it. She placed her right hand on her bag and felt the warm leather. An eighteenth birthday present from her mother. She hadn't seen another purse as practical as that one in the ten years since. She could fit her books and her ballet equipment in it, and it even had secret compartments. She must have a few *reais* left in her wallet. House keys... Where could she sleep tonight? Sunscreen, wristwatch, a telephone book containing all of the addresses and telephone numbers that she knew in the whole wide world... Her good luck necklace... She ran her fingers over her bag, like a pregnant woman feeling her stomach. She felt a bulge. *The City in Crimson Cloak*! The only copy of her novel, with all of her notes, every word she'd written in the last two years, was in that green notebook. The only thing she could say to Rio, the only answer she could give... A monological dialogue... "Forget it," she said to herself in Turkish. "FORGET IT. IT'S NOT WORTH IT."

She undoubtedly heard the terrible explosion at her very ears, but she didn't have time to make sense of it. She'd been lucky. Before she even realized she'd been shot, she fell face-up onto the sidewalk, as if being pulled down to the ground by a heavy mask. Without having to endure unbearable agony, without experiencing the horror of knowing that you are certain to die in a short amount of time, without making a single sound, she met her death. In just the amount of time that it takes for an upright human body to collapse onto the ground... An inconspicuous, unwitnessed, lonely death—just the kind of death that befit her personality. A completely coincidental, completely meaningless death, with no prayers, no hymns, no trumpets involved... Nobody can know if she suffered or not, or if her life passed before her very eyes like a movie reel... Her final, silent scream remained unanswered in the vast ocean of silence.

Patrolmen from the Catete Police Headquarters making their rounds on Monday morning noticed that she still clung onto her bag. And that her eyes were wide open. Not out of fear, or pain, or horror, but more like an expression of mental concentration. As if at that moment, she was trying to explain death itself. In a city called Rio de Janeiro, on an ordinary Sunday convulsing with fireworks, as the sky surrendered itself to darkness once again after the tropical sundown; as the suffocating heat continued its tyrannical reign, despite the ocean breeze; as the women of Rio finished putting on their make-up to go to Sunday dances, out to dinner, or to a concert; as the buses packed full of wet-haired, salt-scented passengers came back from the Copacabana beach; as kiosk workers turned on coffee pots and rolled out kegs of beer for the thirsty travelers journeying through a vast darkness; as street children set out to find their mothers for dinner; as the Blue Hill favela announced to the city that the week's supply of cocaine was now up for sale, and somewhere out there, far away, melancholy choral melodies rang out; she was trying to explain what it was like to die on a street full of junk cars, broken glass, and oil stains. Stunned to be the heroine of a tragedy for the first and last time, to be confronting an indomitable reality one-on-one... Her eyes gaping in a quest of splendid adjectives, crucial images, and the words closest to reality itself. They were trying to convey that single moment, that moment when life shrinks eternally into a spaceless point, and thus expands eternally. Actually, she had died exactly as she had wanted.

About the Author

One of Turkey's most challenging young authors, **Aslı Erdogan** has been a critical success both in Turkey and Europe. A former physicist who abandoned her scientific career for a literary one, Erdogan's first book, the novel *Kabuk Adam* (*The Shell Man*), was published in 1994. She went on to make her mark abroad two years later when she received the Deutsche Welle Prize for her short story "The Wooden Birds." Erdogan has devoted herself to writing full-time since 1996.

From 1998 to 2000 Erdogan, a human rights activist and former Turkish representative of PEN's Writers in Prison Committee, wrote a column for the Turkish newspaper *Radikal* entitled "The Others". Her articles were later collected and published as the book *Bir Yolculuk Ne Zaman Biter* (*When a Journey Ends*). Two of these articles are featured in the 2004 edition of M.E.E.T.'s journal.

Erdogan has also participated in various exhibitions both in Turkey and abroad, and has recently been a featured guest at international literary and arts events such as the Beaux Arts Festival in Brussels, the Kunstfestival in Antwerp, where she read together with Emine Sevgi Özdamar. A piece from her upcoming book was most recently staged by Serra Yılmaz in Italian at the Festival Teatro Europa Mediterraneo in Milan in October of this year.